Praise for Ca

'**A small miracle** – sharp, sl
Nick (

'Part comic romp and part nail-biting thriller ... Castle Freeman writes with **both wit and a deep understanding of the human psyche**, and he does not cheat us out of a dramatic climax.' *Guardian*

'Shares many small-town, big-crime themes with Cormac McCarthy... it is **impossible not to appreciate this**.' *The Times*

'**Wonderful... every paragraph a gem**. Freeman – like Cormac McCarthy, like Annie Proulx – shows us the awkward realness of lives, and does it with humour, with wry perception, with great style.' R. J. Ellory

'Extremely funny... streamlined storytelling, dead-on dialogue and lyrical descriptions of the bleak, woodsy landscape. This is a **meticulous New England miniature, with not a word wasted.**' *Oprah Magazine*

'A fast, memorable read gooey with atmosphere... **a gem that sparkles with sly insight and cuts like a knife.**' *Boston Globe*

'Freeman has a flawless ear for dialogue and a sharp eye for quirky detail ... **Superb**.' *People Magazine*

'A brilliant book – **laconic, spare, stylish and exciting**.' Al Alvarez

'**A small masterpiece of black comedy and suspense** ... If all novels were this good, Americans would read more.' *Kirkus Reviews*

Praise for Castle Freeman

CHILDREN OF THE VALLEY

Castle Freeman

This edition published in 2020 by Farrago,
an imprint of Duckworth Books Ltd
13 Carrington Road, Richmond,
TW10 5AA, United Kingdom

www.farragobooks.com

Print ISBN: 9781788422499
Ebook ISBN: 9781788422482

Cover design by kid-ethic
Cover image: Shutterstock

Have you read them all?

Treat yourself again to the Lucian Wing novels by Castle Freeman –

All That I Have
A local tearaway gets tangled up with big-league criminals on Sheriff Wing's patch.

Old Number Five
Lucian Wing ends up drawing on his last ounces of patience, tact, and – especially – humour.

Children of the Valley
A pair of runaways take refuge in Sheriff Wing's slice of the Vermont countryside.

Turn to the end of this book for a full list of Castle Freeman's books, plus – on the last page – the chance to receive **further background material**.

Contents

1
The De-Escalation of Rhumba

Nine – no, ten – vehicles were parked in front of Krugers', on the grass, in the road, around back in the lane: two deputies, four Staties, including a command car, two ambulances, the Cardiff Fire Department's second-best pumper, and a line truck from the telephone company. The first to arrive had been here for half an hour. Nothing had happened, nothing had changed. So now they were waiting. They were waiting for something to move. They were waiting for me.

I left my truck in the road and walked to them, keeping the cruisers between the house and me. A small house, needed a coat of paint. Needed a coat of paint and a rich owner; wasn't going to get either one. We called the place Krugers'. It had been Krugers' at one time. I didn't know whose it was now; it was rented out. Storey-and-a-half, so hard to see what's going on upstairs. Not good. Tiny yards in front and behind, then woods all around. So no near neighbours. Good.

Dwight Farrabaugh, the state police captain in charge of this action, and the Cardiff fire chief were standing behind the pumper in the road. Normally, an officer of the grade of captain wouldn't turn out for what looked like another no-frills domestic dispute, but in this case firearms were reported to be involved, and so were minor children.

Guns and kids get everybody wound up – everybody, including the press. Therefore, Dwight had favoured us with his presence this morning.

Wingate was there, too. Evidently he had busted out of the old-folks' home and hitched a ride to the action with the chief. I joined them.

'Well, if it ain't The Chill,' said Farrabaugh. 'Where the hell have you been?'

'Goofing off,' I said. 'Like you. Hello, Chief. Where's the new rig?' Cardiff Fire had recently purchased a new pumper. Usually, the volunteers were eager to take it to calls to show it off to the townspeople, who had dug deep to pay for it; but today it had been left at the station.

'Don't want no holes in my brand new truck,' said the fire chief. 'Specially not on account of a piece of shit like Rhumba.'

'Good idea,' I said. 'Thought you'd retired,' I said to Wingate. Wingate shrugged. 'Like you see,' he said.

I looked around. I could see the three Staties just inside the woods. They were watching the house with binoculars. The deputies would be doing the same on the other side. 'So?' I asked. 'What have we got? Rhumba again, I guess?'

'The very same,' said Dwight.

'Rhumba and who else?' I asked.

'The missus. Three of her kids, maybe more. Three we know of: two little, one medium.'

'They're upstairs?'

Dwight nodded.

'We've got eyes?'

'Sure. Missus has a shiner on her as big as a golf ball. She's scroonched into a corner. Kids are under the bed.'

'Smart kids,' I said. 'And Rhumba?'

'Downstairs. He's shoved a big old couch against the front door. He's behind it or near it. He moves around.'

'Back door?' I asked.

'Kitchen. We can be through it and in there in ten seconds. 'Course, that's going in with weight.'

'Right,' I said. 'Let's just take it slow for now. Okay?'

'Here you go again,' said Dwight.

'Just for now,' I said.

'Now means *not long*, right?'

'Of course,' I said. 'Equipment?'

'Shotgun,' said Dwight.

'He says,' said Wingate.

'You've seen it?' I asked.

'Negative,' said Dwight. 'He had one last time. If you recall.'

'I recall,' I said. 'We've got sound?'

'Over there,' said Dwight, and he pointed to the telephone company's truck.

'Well, then,' I said.

***

I sat in the cab of the line truck waiting for Rhumba's connection to patch through and drinking lukewarm coffee from a paper cup. Somehow Wingate had found a coffee pot. Forty years in law enforcement, you may not always get your man, but you always get your coffee. Wingate sat in the cab beside me, listening for the call.

'Hello?' Rhumba's voice came in.

'Earl?' I said. 'Earl, this is Lucian Wing. How are you doing in there?'

'Fuck you,' said Rhumba. He didn't like you to use his real name.

'Okay, Rhumba,' I said. 'Who have you got with you?'

'All of them,' said Rhumba. 'The slut, the brats, the whole nine yards.'

'Three kids, then?' I looked at Wingate. He drank his coffee.

'You're asking me?' said Rhumba. 'You got your assholes falling out of the trees, here, spying around. You tell me who I've got.'

'We see three kids.'

'Ha-ha, then,' said Rhumba. 'There's four. Four and the whore. Ha-ha.'

'Good one,' I said. 'What are you going to do?'

'What do you think?' Rhumba seemed to clear his throat.

'Rhumba?' I pushed him.

Rhumba made a little sound, might have been a cough, might have been a sob. 'I'm going to kill them all,' he said.

'Okay,' I said. 'Okay, Rhumba. Ten-four. You're coming through loud and clear. But nobody's in a hurry, here, right? Let's slow it down. Let's take a breath.'

'You take a breath,' said Rhumba. 'I've told you: this time, I'm doing it.'

'I know you don't want the kids hurt,' I said.

'You've got no fucking idea what I do or don't want,' said Rhumba. 'You say you do, but you don't. You don't know.'

'You're right,' I said. 'I don't know.'

'I've had enough with this thing,' Rhumba went on. 'I have fucking had enough.'

'I know you have, Rhumba,' I said. 'We all know you have. What you've put up with? Anybody would have snapped.'

'I'm snapping now,' said Rhumba. 'I am fucking snapping.'

'I know you are, Rhumba. We all know you are... Uhh ... Hang on a second.'

I turned to Wingate. I covered the phone with my hand. 'He ain't drunk,' I said. 'Don't sound it, anyhow.'

'No,' said Wingate.

'I wish I knew if he's really got something in there, like the other time,' I said.

'I wish you knew, too, sheriff,' said Wingate. 'Young Dwight will be getting restless. Pretty soon, time to guess and go.'

'Guess and go,' I said.

'My guess?' said Wingate. 'He's got nothing.'

'How do you know?'

'I don't know. I knew, it wouldn't be a guess.'

'Well,' I said, 'I've got to go someplace with him.'

'Try a new deck,' said Wingate.

'I could do that,' I said. 'But would it work?'

'One way to find out.'

'Earl?' I said into the phone. 'You there, Earl?'

'Fuck you,' said Rhumba.

'We've been talking, out here, trying to recall. That place?'

'Place? What place?'

'Your place, there. Where you're at. You rent, right?'

'Say *what*?'

'Your place. Your house. Where you live. You rent it, right? From – is it still Krugers?'

'What are you talking about?' Rhumba asked. 'Did you hear me? I said – I said I'm going to kill them all. I've had enough, and I'm going to do it.'

'I got that, Earl,' I said. 'But I'm asking you about your house. Are you renters? Who's your landlord? Is it still Krugers?'

'No,' said Rhumba. 'The landlord's Brown.'

'Brown?' I asked him. 'Is that the same Brown had the camp up on Diamond? His brother was killed in Vietnam? Wendell Brown?'

'Who? What?'

'Your landlord, Earl,' I said. 'Help me out, here, can't you? Wasn't he the one whose brother was killed? They had that camp. Brad McKinnon got a ten-pointer up there years ago?'

'That's right,' said Rhumba. 'My dad was there. Said it was the god damnedest buck he ever saw. But his name's not Wendell. It's Wayne.'

'Who is?' I asked him.

'The guy that had the camp, where McKinnon—'

'What camp?'

'The camp we've been talking about,' Rhumba said. 'The camp on Diamond.'

'Oh,' I said. '*That* camp.'

'What other camp is there?'

'Quite a few.'

'Fuck you, Lucian,' said Rhumba.

'I was just asking,' I said. 'Just trying to get us clear. You know me: I like things clear.'

'Lucian?' Rhumba asked.

'Yes, Earl.'

'This is a pretty fucked-up situation, here, you know it?'
'I know.'
'Sometimes,' Rhumba said. 'Things get pretty fucked up.'
'They do,' I said. 'Listen: you ready to step out here? See what we can do? Talk a little, here? You don't feel right, you can always go back inside. No funny stuff.'
'Just fucked up,' said Rhumba. 'Hang on a minute, Lucian.' The phone clicked off. We could hear bumping and scraping from inside the house as Rhumba moved his barricade couch out of the way of the front door. Wingate dumped the remains of his coffee out the window of the telephone company's truck. 'Done deal,' he said. 'I saw it, too, you know. That buck. That was a hell of an animal. Where are you headed now?'
'Back to the office, I guess,' I said.
'Drop me at the place?' Wingate asked me.

***

'The Chill Rides Again,' said Dwight Farrabaugh. 'Another satisfied customer.'
Rhumba sat in the back of one of the Staties' cruisers being interviewed. Two deputies had gone over the house: no shotgun. No other firearms. Good. A couple from the state's Department of Children and Families were talking to Mrs. Rhumba and the kids. Four kids, as Rhumba had said. All of them apparently okay. Good, again.
Dwight was wrapping up. He slapped me on the back. 'Thanks, Lucian,' he said. 'I don't know how you do it.'
'Natural gift for improvisation,' I said.
'Natural gift for bullshit, more like,' said Dwight. He turned to his command car, ready to be on his way.

Well, he's more right than wrong, Dwight, ain't he? But the bullshit ain't the main thing. The bullshit is a means to an end. The end is boredom, and the end is impatience. The end is fatigue. People backed right up to the wall, like Rhumba, expend a lot of energy. They tire quickly. They want above all for something to happen, anything. They've climbed up to the top of the flagpole, and now they don't know what's next. They don't know where to go. All they know is, they want action.

They want decision. They want an event. My job is to see they don't get one. Instead, they get the bullshit. They get irrelevance. They get talk. The talk wanders around from no-place to no-place and back again. Pretty soon, your subject is so bored, so dazed by the storm of bullshit, that, to stop it, he climbs down from the flagpole. He goes quietly. It's a method. It ain't exciting, but it often works, and, when it works, everybody walks away.

De-escalation is what scholars of law enforcement call the method. Dwight Farrabaugh and others call it *chilling*. Wingate don't call it anything, but it was Wingate who taught the method to me. He's still teaching it, as you can see, and, although I'm glad to have his advice, I'll admit sometimes I wish he'd leave off. Wingate was sheriff of our county forty years. He hired me for a deputy, and I took over for him when he retired ten–twelve years ago. Pretty soon, I learned Wingate had his own ideas on retirement. Retirement was a state of mind, not a fact, and it was a state of mind Wingate was never in. Wingate has retired more times than Frank Sinatra. The more he retires, the more he comes back. And who's going to tell him he can't? If Frank Sinatra shows up in Las Vegas and says he'd like to sing a couple of the old favourites, is Las Vegas going to tell him to go away? Frank built Las Vegas. Frank owned Las Vegas. He'll sing if he damned wants to. Same with Wingate in our valley. Now, inability to retire may be the only way Wingate's like Frank Sinatra, I guess. I can't think of any others. But, then, I don't know Frank. Maybe there's more.

I left Wingate at the entrance to Steep Mountain House. He got down out of the truck and stood for a minute with his hand on the door.

'How's Clementine?' Wingate asked me.

'Tip-top,' I said. 'Never better.'

'Uh-huh,' said Wingate. 'Well, keep your spoon clean, young fellow. Good job on Rhumba. We'll see you.' He turned and walked toward the building. He went slowly, and I saw he was using his cane today. Wingate's not a kid.

2
Sources

The sheriff's department, and my office, had recently been moved out of the county courthouse where they belonged and into the old District 4 school in South Cardiff. The town had built a nice new elementary school. The old one was too small, too dilapidated, and too dangerously in violation of too many codes to be worth keeping up – so they gave it to our department to use until it fell down. If people still had outdoor privies, they would have put us in one of those. Sheriff's departments, at least in this state, are the poor relations of law enforcement. We're at the very end of the soup line, so when we reach the pot there ain't much left beyond bones and grey, greasy water.

When I got back to the office after the de-escalation of Rhumba and getting Wingate home, I found a long black town car in our little lot, a boat that belonged double-parked on Fifth Avenue, not waiting at a plain, out at the elbows cop-shop off in the woods. There was a driver, too, I saw, a uniformed driver: black suit, white shirt, dark tie, peaked cap. When I pulled in beside the town car, he left the driver's seat and opened one of the rear doors to let his passenger climb out.

The passenger was a tall man in his fifties, heavy, well set-up, wearing a dark pin-striped suit and a red silk tie. He ought to have been double-parked on Fifth Avenue, too. When I approached him, he said, 'You're the sheriff?'

I nodded. 'Lucian Wing,' I said. I held out my hand, but this man didn't want good manners. Instead, he handed me a business card.

CARL
ARMENTROUT
Special Assistant
LORD ENTERPRISES
LTD.
New York   Los Angeles   London

'Mr. Armentrout,' I said, 'you're off your beat, aren't you?'

'We'll go into your office,' said Armentrout.

Uh-oh. All business today. Okay. Sure. Why not?

I let Carl Armentrout go before me into the building and past the front desk, where Evelyn, the despatcher on duty, was at her station. When she got a look at Mr. Armentrout, her eyebrows flew up her forehead like a pair of partridges flushed from a thicket. We don't see a lot of Armentrout's class of trade at our little stand. I winked at Evelyn and showed Armentrout down the hallway to my door. In the office I pointed Armentrout to the visitor's chair and started around the desk to my own, but, 'Hold it, Sheriff,' said Armentrout. 'Close the door.'

Okay. Fine. I went to the office door, shut it, and took my place behind the desk. I laid Armentrout's card on the blotter in front of my chair.

Armentrout nodded at the card. He cleared his throat. 'Sheriff,' he said, 'I represent Rex Lord, in New York. You know the name.'

'I can't say I do,' I told him. 'Who's Rex Lord?'

'Come on, Sheriff. Lord Enterprises?'

I shook my head.

'Lord Properties?'

I shook my head again. 'We're pretty far out in the woods up here, Mr. Armentrout,' I said. 'We miss things.'

Armentrout gave me a thin smile. 'I didn't know you could get that far out in the woods,' he said.

'Lucky for us,' I said, 'you can help me. Who is Rex Lord?' But Armentrout flicked his hand. 'I don't have time to take you through *Who's Who*, here, Sheriff,' he said. 'Suffice to say, Mr. Lord is a very important man. He's a very powerful man. He's also a very worried man. Which is why I'm here today.'

'What's he worried about?'

'His stepdaughter, Pamela.'

'Why's he worried about her?'

'She's missing,' said Armentrout. 'Nobody knows where she is. Nobody's heard from her.'

'How old's the girl?' I asked him.

'Seventeen.'

'How long's she been missing?'

'Since Tuesday.'

'Three–four days, then,' I said. 'Seventeen years old. That would get a fellow worried, all right. You think she's around here?'

'We think it's possible.'

'Why?'

'Sources.'

I looked at him.

'Her school,' said Armentrout. 'She goes to a boarding school near Boston. St. Bartholomew's. They broke for the summer last week. Pamela was to spend the vacation with her stepfather in New York. Mr. Lord's driver went up to get the girl and her things and take them back to the city. She wasn't there. She wasn't anywhere around the school. Her things were in her room, but she was gone.'

'What did you do then?'

'Checked her friends. St. Bartholomew's is a top school, Sheriff. Students go there from all over the country, from all over the world. At first we thought she'd gone home with her roommate, to L.A. She hadn't. Then we thought she'd gone to visit a classmate in Dallas. I flew down there. No. She's gone.'

'What's your idea, then?' I asked Armentrout. 'Do you think she's been taken? Abducted? Harmed? Worse?'

'No,' said Armentrout. 'We think she's safe. She's run away.'

'From her stepfather?'

'They aren't on good terms,' said Armentrout.

'You talk to the police in Mass.?' I asked him.

'No,' said Armentrout. 'No police. Mr. Lord prefers to be discreet. You understand me, Sheriff? Discreet? He prefers the police not be involved in any way.'

'I'm the police,' I said.

Armentrout gave me the chilly little smile again. 'We feel you're safe,' he said.

'Because I'm small-time,' I said.

'You said it, Sheriff, not I.'

'Your missing girl got a mother?'

'Her mother's not part of this.'

'How do you know? Have you talked to her?'

'She and Mr. Lord don't speak.'

'Lot of that going around, isn't there?' I said. 'Daughter doesn't speak to dad. Dad doesn't speak to mom. Nobody speaks to the cops. That's a lot of not speaking, wouldn't you say?'

Now it was Armentrout's turn to look at me. He was silent.

'Okay,' I said. 'I'm still waiting to find out why you think the Girl – what's her name, did you say?'

'Pamela.'

'Why you're looking for Pamela up here.'

'A friend of hers at school comes from here,' said Armentrout.

'Boy friend? Girl friend?'

'Boy.'

'What's his name?'

'March,' said Armentrout. 'Duncan March.'

'Buster March's kid,' I said.

'You know the boy?'

'I know his father. Know Dunc, too, sure, I do. Big, strong kid. Football player.'

'And the father?'

'Buster.'

'Buster,' said Armentrout. 'So, is the boy with his father?'

'I doubt it,' I said. 'Buster's mostly on the road. You could say he isn't much of a dad. No, Dunc's at school. He goes to school out of state.'

'I know that, Sheriff,' said Armentrout. 'He goes to St. Bartholomew's, too. Football's big there.'

'I know it is,' I said. 'I know that school.'

'You do?' asked Armentrout. 'St. Bartholomew's? I wouldn't have thought you would, Sheriff. How do you know it? I doubt you're an alumnus.'

'No,' I said.

'How, then?'

'Sources,' I said.

We sat there for a minute. People like Mr. Armentrout and his boss get into my work from time to time. Too often for me. They think, when they come up here from the city, that they've brought the city with them. They're big in the city, they rule the city, and they reckon that means they ought to rule up here, too. Why not? It's all based on money, ain't it, and it's the same money, US dollars, working both places. They reckon we're all doormen, headwaiters, taxi drivers, chauffeurs, nannies, housekeepers, gardeners, masseurs, escorts, butlers, bartenders, tailors, and so on, just like the people they pay for down-country. And they're right, I guess, in a way. It's all the same money, for sure, and they're the ones who have got it. Plus, they're free citizens, voters, and taxpayers. We serve them. That's our job. Still, it ain't all on their side. We can't make them go away, and we can't make them change. But we can make them wait.

'What is it you want me to do, here, Mr. Armentrout?' I asked.

'I should have thought that was obvious, Sheriff,' said Armentrout. 'Find the girl. This is the wilderness up here. It's the woods. We're not Indians, Sheriff. We can't find the girl in the woods. You can. You know the woods. We want you to find Pamela. That, or prove she's not to be found, not around here.'

'Tough to prove a thing's *not* around, isn't it?'

Armentrout gave me a look of growing impatience and dislike. 'Look, Sheriff,' he said. 'I'm not going to get into some half-assed philosophical discussion with you today. You know what we want. I can tell you, as well, that Mr. Lord is in a position to show his gratitude.'

'I bet he is,' I said.

'I mean, show it in generous ways.'

'I understand you,' I said.

'Extremely generous,' said Armentrout.

'Good for him.'

'So?' Armentrout pressed. But I was having too much fun to quit right yet. I returned to his business card, on the desk before me.

'"Special Assistant," it says here. What's that mean? Are you part of the family, you a relative? Friend? Investigator? Are you maybe a cop, yourself?'

'I'm an attorney,' said Armentrout.

'An attorney?' I said. 'Is that right? You know, I thought you might be. I just had a little feeling an attorney might be what you were. Are you with a firm in New York, then?'

'No,' said Armentrout. 'I'm on retainer to Mr. Lord. Exclusive retainer.'

'"On retainer?" I wish somebody would put me on retainer. If possible a generous fellow like your boss.'

'You're not funny, Sheriff,' said Armentrout.

'I know it,' I said. 'I can't help myself. Okay, Mr. Armentrout. My deputies and I will look for your girl, we'll go to her friends and family, we'll go to young March, supposing he's not missing, too. We'll beat the bushes, like you want us to. If she's alive and if she's in the valley, we'll probably find her pretty quick. It's hard to get lost, even in the woods, believe it or not. If we find her, then what?'

'You call me. I won't be far away. I'll be right here, ready to take Pamela home to New York, to her father.'

'What if she doesn't want to go?' I asked Armentrout. 'You said they don't get on.'

'Not your concern,' said Armentrout.

'What if I decide it is?'

'You won't. Remember what I said about Mr. Lord? His power? His gratitude? The power's far-reaching. More to the point, for you, now, is the gratitude. The gratitude's contingent. You understand me, Sheriff? Find the girl. Don't let her throw herself away on some woodchuck.'

'Careful, Mr. Armentrout,' I said. 'You're in Woodchuck Central, now, you know. Woodchucks is mostly what we've got, up here.'

***

I stood in the doorway of the sheriff's building and watched Carl Armentrout's long car turn out of our lot and away. Deputy Treat joined me. He had driven in from patrol while Armentrout and I were talking.

'Who was that?' Treat asked me.

'A concerned citizen,' I said.

'Concerned about what?' asked Treat. 'Did I write him up? I don't recall the car.'

'No, no,' I said. 'Don't worry. He's not mad, he's anxious. His daughter's AWOL.'

'Here?'

'He thinks maybe. Did you happen to talk to his driver, at all?'

'Tried,' said Treat. 'He didn't have a lot to say. Britisher. Wanted to know where he could get a draft Guinness. I said Boston. Then I told him the inn had Guinness in bottles. He told me not to be silly.'

'Don't sound as though you got a lot of useful information from the driver, then,' I said.

'It doesn't, does it?' said Treat.

Deputy Roland Treat had been in our department for a year. I'd had my doubts about him at first: a single man, quiet, neat, well-spoken, kept to himself. I couldn't fault him. He knew his job. He worked hard, he caught on fast, he was willing to go the extra mile, the extra day. More, Deputy Treat seemed not to think his badge was a licence to boss everybody around and get them pissed off. A most promising young man. I'd hired him out of the US Navy, just as Wingate had hired me. Wingate liked Navy men, he said, because, as we were stuck in the only landlocked state in New England, sailors wouldn't ever feel really at home, and therefore they wouldn't get to feel they knew everything. They'd be alert. They'd be watchful.

'So, he wants us to find his kid?' Treat asked me.

'Wants us to look for her, anyway,' I said. 'Do you know Duncan March at all?'

'The orphan?'

'I don't know if he's an orphan, exactly,' I said.

'He's got no parents, I thought,' said the deputy.

'He's got a father,' I said. 'It's true Buster ain't around too much. Dunc's mom's out West.'

'So,' said the deputy, 'he's an orphan, right?'

'I ought to put you on this,' I said. 'You already know all about it.'

'How's Duncan come in?' asked Treat.

'He's boyfriends–girlfriends with the missing daughter, I guess,' I said. 'They're at the same school in Mass.'

'You want me to take a ride out to March's? See if Buster's in town? See if he knows anything about Dunc?'

'Not today,' I said. 'I've got to get a little background, first. A little context.'

'How are you going to do that?' Deputy Treat asked me.

'Sources,' I said.

3
Ride a White Horse

One source, anyway. Quitting time, I drove out to South Devon to pay a call on Addison Jessup. Before his retirement, Addison had had a law practice in town. Another lawyer, then, though not like Mr. Armentrout – or I hoped not. Addison had also, one time and another, held about every state and local office going, including representative to the Vermont house and senate, county prosecutor – even lieutenant governor. Addison had a window on the world outside the valley that nobody else I knew could begin to match. For example, Addison had gone to St. Bartholomew's, the same high-class boarding school from which the runaway girl, Pamela Lord, had made off. He was connected down there, too. In fact, it was Addison who had led the school authorities to offer Duncan March an athletic scholarship for the sake of getting him out of his situation at home, where he suffered under the heavy thumb of Buster, never better than an absent father, but an absent father who was not nearly absent enough.

Addison had lobbied St. Bartholomew's on Duncan's behalf, and he had largely (and anonymously) underwritten Duncan's scholarship.

Addison had the wallet for that, and for more, maybe. If I was going to be dealing with my new friend Mr. Armentrout and his powerful boss, then Addison was the best card I held. He was also my father-in-law.

On my way to Addison's, I stopped at the state store and picked up a fifth of White Horse Scotch. Addison had a taste for the stuff – in the same way that Count Dracula had a taste for Type O-Positive. Deputy Treat had offered to ride along, but I wouldn't let him. I wasn't sure the deputy's liver, young as it was, could stand a visit to Addison.

I found Addison at his place, in the room he called his office; though I never understood why he called it that, seeing he didn't do anything in his office besides read (and drink). Addison's a reader.

'Rex Lord?' said Addison. 'Well, of course I've read about him. I've met him, too, though it was years ago. In New York. Rex was only an ambitious newcomer then, strictly minor league: couldn't have had more than a few hundred million between him and the soup kitchen. It can't have been easy for Rex in those days.'

'How did you know him?'

'I knew his wife – or the woman who became his wife.'

'The missing girl's mother?'

'Probably. If it's the same wife. Lord's had several. Carlotta Campbell. Beautiful woman. Charming. Smart. Funny. Loved a good party. Drank us all under the table. Everybody was a little in love with Lottie.'

'But Rex Lord got her,' I said. 'He married her.'

'Eventually,' said Addison. 'Not right off. Before Lord, Lottie married a guy called Roger DeMorgan. State Department man. Diplomat. Lottie figured she'd soon be the ambassador's lady somewhere fun. Good plan, except that DeMorgan was a genuine moron. I mean, the real thing. Looked good in striped pants, but that was it. Lottie saw this, took stock, dumped Roger, and moved on. Only hitch? They'd had a kid, a daughter. What's her name?'

'Pamela?' I said.

'That's it,' said Addison. 'Pammy. Anyway, couple of years after Carlotta divorced DeMorgan, she married Lord.'

'You know the girl at all?' I asked Addison.

'Never seen her,' he said.

'You ain't in touch with her, then?'

'Of course not. Why would I be?'

'You wouldn't,' I said. 'I'm asking because she's gone missing. The girl, Pamela. She's supposed to be in school. She ain't. Her stepfather thinks she might be up here. She and her stepfather ain't friendly.'

Addison nodded.

'What happened to the girl's father, the State Department fellow?' I asked.

'Last I heard, he was something in the embassy in Mexico City,' said Addison.

'I thought you said he was so dumb.'

'He is,' said Addison, 'but he hasn't let it hold him back. There are a good many like that at State.'

'I believe you,' I said, 'but I'm still on Rex Lord. Who *is* Lord, exactly?'

'Exactly? I don't know, *exactly*. I doubt Lord does. Basically, he owns things,' said Addison.

'You mean, he's in real estate?' I asked.

'Kind of,' said Addison.

'He's an investor?'

'Kind of,' said Addison.

'A speculator?' I said.

'Kind of,' said Addison. 'Look, Lucian, you ask what Rex Lord does. He does whatever he likes. He does anything that makes a great deal of money. *Anything*, you understand? He's one of the wealthy unincarcerated.'

'What's that mean?' I asked.

'It means Lord ought to be in prison, but he isn't, he never has been, and he never will be,' said Addison. 'The Gospels say the poor ye have always with ye, but they forgot about the rich. The rich ye have always with ye, too. They're like cockroaches.'

When Addison starts quoting scripture, it's almost time to slip an extra ice cube into his White Horse and change the subject. I didn't have much longer.

'He's got this helper, too,' I said. I passed Carl Armentrout's card to Addison. '"Special Assistant," it says. He's Lord's point man up here, like.'

Addison looked the card over briefly and handed it back to me. He shook his head.

'Don't worry about him,' said Addison. 'He's only the scout.'

'Scout?' I said. 'He's no scout. He's a big-shot lawyer. He's on exclusive retainer or some such to Lord. That means Lord's his only client, right?'

'That's what it means,' said Addison. 'So what?'

'Pretty fancy stuff, ain't it?' I asked him. 'Having your own private lawyer?'

'Not to worry, Lucian,' said Addison. 'A man like Rex Lord has lawyers to mow his lawn, lawyers to walk his dog. It's not the lawyers you need to look out for. It's the people who come after the lawyers.'

'What people?'

'You'll see, if you don't find the girl,' said Addison. 'Lord and his kind always double-team. Double, at the least. If they've got a lawyer watching you, then they'll have somebody else watching the lawyer, and probably a third watching the watcher. Only, the last ones won't be lawyers. They'll have other means. They'll be more, ah, forthright. Best thing? Find the girl, Lucian. Find her quickly. What about another drink?'

'I'm all set, thanks,' I said. 'I'll call her school tomorrow.'

Addison laughed at that. 'St. Bartholomew's?' he said. 'Don't waste your time. They'll have no idea where she is.'

'It's a boarding school, ain't it?' I asked him. 'The kids live there, don't they? The school has to keep track of them, then.'

'Dream on, Lucian,' said Addison. 'Oh, maybe at one time they did. No more. Nowadays, everybody runs wild. Schools like Bart's are like game preserves. They're like the national parks. The students are the bison, the elk. They go where they like, do what they like. The faculty works for the park. They don't get too close to the students. They watch them through binoculars. That's all they do. By now, it's all they can do.

'I blame coeducation,' Addison went on. 'In my day, Bart's was a boys' school. It was a maximum security institution, top to bottom. Talk about incarceration? They shackled us to our beds at night.'

'The hell they did,' I said.

'Well, they would have,' said Addison. 'They should have. They wanted to. And rightly so. We were savages, we boys. We were young wolves, young hyenas. The school let girls in because they thought girls would humanise us. It did the opposite. It made wolves and hyenas of the girls, too. The school tried to put out a fire by pouring gasoline on it. Look here: have another round?'

'Maybe a short one.'

'That's my boy,' said Addison, reaching for the bottle. 'How's Clemmie?' he asked me. 'Never better,' I said. 'Truly? All's well at home?'

'Oh, yes,' I said. 'Very well.'

'Good, good,' said Addison. 'Glad to hear it.'

He poured us each a small one. 'As for Lord,' he went on, 'well, I see his position. If Clemmie had ever taken off like that, I probably would have called out the cavalry, too. Any cavalry.'

'Lord's man says he'll pay the big money to find her,' I said.

'Of course, he will,' said Addison.

'Says Lord don't want her to throw herself away,' I told Addison.

'No,' said Addison.

'He don't want her to throw herself away on a woodchuck, his man said,' I told Addison.

'That would be a terrible thing,' said Addison.

4
Cow Parsnip

Clementine Templeton Jessup Wing, my bride, my love, my destiny, snatched up a coffee mug from the kitchen table, cocked her slender arm, and fired the mug across the room, straight at my nose. I dodged to my right and caught it in my left hand. 'Ball one!' I cried. Clemmie picked up another mug and hurled it after the first. I caught that one with my right. 'Ball two!' I called.

'Damn you, Lucian,' Clemmie hissed.

'You got the speed,' I told her. 'You want to work on control.'

'Damn you, damn you, *damn* you,' Clemmie raged. Having nothing left to throw, she collapsed into a chair and sat, beating the table with her pretty fists.

I approached her and set the two mugs down on the table, then slid them across to the end farthest from Clemmie. I sat down beside her.

'A thing I've always liked about you?' I told Clemmie. 'You don't throw like a girl. You don't push the ball, or the crockery, or whatever it is. You whip it. You *whip* it over. I admire that. I do.'

Clemmie let out a little squeak, but she kept her head down so I wouldn't see she was laughing. Then she looked up at me. She pointed at the coffee mugs on the table. 'You're lucky that wasn't a gun,' she said.

'You don't like guns,' I reminded her.

'I could get to like them,' Clemmie said.

The telephone on the wall rang. I went to pick it up as Clemmie rose from her place and left the kitchen, slamming the door behind her with a loud bang.

'Sheriff Wing,' I said into the phone.

'Sheriff? It's Treat. Is that you?'

'Right here,' I said.

'Is everything okay? I thought I heard a gunshot.'

'All secure, Deputy,' I said. 'That wasn't a gunshot. That was Mrs. Wing making her point in a family conference. Everything's fine.'

'Oh,' said Deputy Treat. 'Oh, okay.'

'What can I do for you, Deputy?' I asked Treat.

'Had a call from a Mrs. Truax. She lives out in Gilead, past the dam.'

'I know where she lives,' I told Treat. 'And she ain't Mrs. She's *Miz.* Ms. Truax. Get it?'

'Oh,' said Treat. 'Oh, okay. Ms. Truax. Anyway, she's pretty upset. She says somebody is growing pot in her woods. Got a whole field of it, she says. She wants you to investigate.'

'Nobody's growing anything in her woods,' I said. 'Go out there, show the flag, get her to give you a cup of coffee, get her calmed down.'

'She wants you, Sheriff,' Treat said. 'She insists.'

'She sure does,' I said. 'Okay, Deputy. I'll meet you out there.'

'I'm going, too?'

'You bet,' I said. 'You haven't made Ms. Truax's acquaintance yet, have you? It's high time. Besides, I might need backup. Don't forget your service weapon.'

***

I drove down off our hill and turned north on the river road. In the fields were numbers of those grey and white gulls that turn up from time to time on open land, seabirds 150 miles from the nearest sea. Where do they come from? Where do they think they are? What do they think they're doing so far from home?

Clemmie and I had gotten into it earlier about her deck: the deck she wanted built on the rear of our little house on Cardiff Hill. I had promised to build the thing myself. What's putting up a deck? Sawing boards and banging nails. No need to pay some thief of a builder. I'd do the job. Easy.

Clemmie wouldn't have it. She wanted a proper deck, she said, not something that looked like it had been thrown together by a gang of intoxicated chimps. We'd get Rory O'Hara's crew, she said.

I told her not to be silly. I'd carpenter her damn deck. What did we need Rory for? Unless… Wait a minute… *Unless* we needed Rory, because Clemmie and Rory had been sweethearts back in junior high school? Did that juvenile flame still burn? Or was there another point, as well? Did we need Rory's crew so Clemmie could get a good look at the college boys Rory hired for summer walking around without their shirts. Was that it?

'Be careful, Lucian,' said Clemmie. Then she said maybe if I looked better without my shirt, she'd let me build her deck.

I told her, yes, those young fellows did look good without their shirts. I might even have suggested that they looked better without their shirts than, say, she did without hers. Now, that was not true, not in any way, not for a minute, but you have to take the shot when it's there, and I thought that was a pretty good one – good enough, anyway, to make Clemmie pick up her coffee mug and start firing.

Clemmie's high-spirited.

***

When I got to Truax's, I found Deputy Treat there ahead of me. He was getting a going-over from Constance Truax. Seeing me, she turned and came stamping up to my truck, walking with a bamboo ski pole which she used as a crutch and brandished like a sabre. I hadn't had time to turn my motor off before she started in on me. Behind her, Treat was grinning and shaking his head.

'This is intolerable, Sheriff,' said Ms. Truax. 'Someone is growing Contraband – someone is growing *narcotics* – on my property. It's an outrage. What do you propose to do?'

'You found some plants?' I asked her.

'*Some?* I found a forest.'

'Okay,' I said. 'Take it easy. Let's have a look.'

Ms. Truax led us around her house, across the backyard, to an old logging track that went uphill into the woods. Before we'd gone far, she began to labour, and puff, and lean on her ski pole. I tried to take her elbow, but she shook me off.

'Get up here much?' I asked her.

'No,' said Ms. Truax. 'I thought I heard something in the woods, some music, like a flute or a recorder. I came to investigate. It's not far now.'

The track levelled off, and we came into a wet, open, logged-over area where the sun got in and brush grew rank on both sides of the way.

'There,' said Ms. Truax, pointing with her ski pole.

Ahead on the right, a large, lofty brake of olive-green growth waved in the air. The stand was seven or eight feet tall with broad, spreading leaves, and it grew like a high hedge or fence along the logging track.

'Look at that,' said Ms. Truax. 'There must be thirty plants. They're enormous.'

'Thirty, easy,' I said. 'And they're big, all right. Big, healthy plants. One thing, though...'

'What's that?' Ms. Truax demanded.

'They ain't pot,' I said.

'What do you mean? Of course they are. What else could they be?'

'Tell her, Deputy,' I said to Treat.

'Cow parsnip, I'd say,' said the deputy. '*Heracleum*.'

'That's preposterous,' said Ms. Truax. She stabbed the point of her ski pole into the ground at her feet.

'Cow parsnip,' I told her. 'Also called hogweed. It looks like pot, I guess, if you don't know what pot looks like – but it ain't.'

'And you know this, how?'

'We see a fair amount of the real thing in our work,' I said. 'Don't we, Deputy?'

'A fair amount,' said Treat.

'We're trained to spot it,' I went on. 'And we're trained to spot the look-alikes, same as we're trained on fake money, fake driver's licences, fake alibis, fake whiskers, fake ID, fake guns – you know.'

'So you're saying all this just grew here?' Ms. Truax asked. 'Nobody planted it? Nobody tended it?'

'It just grew, yes, ma'am,' I said.

Ms. Truax speared the ground again with her pole.

'Well, then,' she asked. 'How do you account for this?'

She turned and charged off along the logging trace, past the patch of hogweed, for another fifty yards or so, where we left the logged-over area and got into the woods again. Deputy Treat and I followed her. Soon Ms. Truax stopped and pointed ahead with her ski pole to an orange pup tent that had been pitched under a big pine. Campfire ring of blackened stones in front. Little pile of broken pine branches for firewood. All very orderly. No trash.

I raised the tent flap, and the deputy and I looked in. 'Pretty cosy,' said Treat. So it was. There was a single sleeping bag, rolled up and stowed neatly in a corner; a shopping bag with some canned chilli, beans, soup, and so on; a gallon bottle of spring water, two-thirds full.

Finally, a single back pack, in it, clothes including two bras and two pairs of women's underpants. At the bottom of the pack, a long silver tube with keys that had to be the flute Ms. Truax had heard; also an old child's toy, a stuffed rabbit wearing a blue coat and short an ear; and a paperback book: *Last Poems*, by W. B. Yeats.

'I heard the flute,' said Ms. Truax.

'When?' I asked her.

'A couple of days ago, first. I couldn't imagine what they were doing.'

'They?'

'They, he, she – I don't know. Do you think there are more than one of them?'

'I don't know, either,' I said. 'But, you take the size of the tent, the single sleeping bag: if there's more than one of them, I hope they're good friends.'

Ms. Truax nodded and favoured the deputy and me with a tight smile, her first of the day, as far as I knew. Maybe the week.

'Yes,' she said. 'And I thought they were tending a marijuana field. They're only campers.'

'I don't know what they are,' I said. 'But if they're up here trying to get high smoking hogweed, then there had better be a bunch of them. They'll need the company. They're in for a long wait.'

'If you say so, Sheriff,' said Ms. Truax.

'When you first came up here,' I asked her, 'you found the hogweed, you found the camp. Nobody was around? Whoever it was, was away?'

'That's right.'

'Did you wait for somebody to get back? Did you come back yourself, another day?'

'No, Sheriff,' said Ms. Truax.

'Why not?' I asked her. 'I'd think you'd want to find out who's in your woods.'

'It's not my job to find that out, Sheriff,' said Constance Truax. 'It's your job.'

***

'Yeats?' Addison said. 'Really?'

'That's right,' I said. 'W. T. Yeats.'

'W. B.,' said Addison. 'Good old Yeats. The last great poet in English, many think. I might agree with them. You?'

'I wouldn't know,' I said.

'Never heard of Yeats?'

I shook my head.

'Irishman,' said Addison. 'Well, Anglo-Irish. Genius. Peculiar fellow. Most peculiar.'

'Irish?' I asked him. 'Probably rode the booze pretty hard, then, don't you bet? The Irish like the stuff, you know. That will get you peculiar.'

'I wouldn't know,' said Addison. 'You found the book in the tent along with some other stuff?'

'Yes,' I said. 'Underwear. A beat-up stuffed rabbit in a blue coat. A flute.'

'A rabbit in a blue coat?' Addison asked me.

'That's right. A toy rabbit, you know.'

'You're pretty sure whoever left them is Pamela? The runaway from Bart's?'

'Who else would it be?' I asked him.

'I don't know,' said Addison. 'Anybody. I'll give you one thing, though. The Yeats. The flute. Peter Rabbit. Whoever's up there isn't your grandma's dope-farmer. I'll give you that.'

5
Big John

'Lucian? Cola Hitchcock.'

'Cola, I'm just getting out of the shower, here. Can I call you right back?'

'He don't care if you're a little wet,' said Cola. ''Long as you're clean.'

'Who don't?'

'John. He's out.'

'Jesus Christ!' I said.

'He won't help you this time,' said Cola. 'It's John, all right. Gracie thought she saw him on the road yesterday. Now he's up here in the woods behind me. He's got a couple yards' length of chain around his neck that the free end's hung up on a stump. He's stuck good, but he's thrashing and crashing around in there so you can't get near him.'

'Call Herbie,' I said.

'Did,' said Cola. 'No answer, no machine. I think they're in Florida.'

'Call the caretaker.'

'Who would that be?' Cola asked me. 'Herbie fired AJ.'

'Call Fish and Wildlife.'

'Tried them, too,' Cola said. 'They say this ain't a wild animal. They can't act.'

'The hell it ain't a wild animal,' I said.

'That's what I told them,' Cola said. 'Don't matter. Their hands are tied, they say.'

'Okay, then, call Homer. He's constable. Constable's the dog officer.'

'My first call,' Cola said. 'Homer says it ain't a dog. It ain't a pet. It ain't livestock, not really. He can't get involved, officially, but he offered to come help out.'

'Call the Staties,' I said. 'Call Farrabaugh.'

'Did,' said Cola.

'What did he say?'

'He laughed.'

'Jesus Christ,' I said again.

'You about dripped dry yet?' Cola asked me.

'I guess I'd better be, hadn't I? Okay, Cola, I'm on my way.'

I got dressed and went downstairs. Clemmie was at the stove. Sweet and smooth as honey this morning. I went to her and gave her a squeeze and a kiss on her fragrant hair. Then I started for the door. 'See you,' I said.

'No breakfast?' Clemmie asked me.

'No time.'

'Coffee? It's all made.'

'Are you serving it today, or are you throwing it?'

'Hah,' said Clemmie. 'Order some, and find out.'

'Not me,' I said. 'See you tonight.'

***

Twenty minutes later, I turned in at the front of Cola's salvage yard outside Dead River Settlement. I left the truck and picked my way carefully toward the shop, stepping over and around the fenders, bumpers, engines, axles, transmissions, drive trains, differentials, chassis, radiators, gas-tanks, and other parts that made up Cola's rusty, slow-moving stock in trade. There was no visible plan or principle to Cola's junk; but you could say with some confidence that ninety percent of it had at one time been on an automobile of one species or another.

Cola called his shop Dead River Recovery, but what and how much was ever in fact recovered, Cola himself couldn't have told you.

As I approached the shop, the door opened, and Cola came out to meet me. I saw he was wearing his US Army infantryman's steel helmet on his head and his heavy old army .45 Colt automatic pistol in a holster on his government-issue web belt. Cola's hobby was World War II, whose paraphernalia he collected. What he had in mind today wasn't clear. The sidearm and gunbelt might have been connected with our mission, or they might have been connected with some other mission, or they might have been connected with keeping Cola's pants up. You couldn't tell. Cola had his own circuitry, it looked like, his own switches. Sometimes, they worked pretty much like yours and mine. Sometimes, they didn't.

'Follow me,' said Cola.

We bushwhacked through the woods behind Cola's for a hundred yards, until Cola halted and pointed ahead to a big beech tree that had fallen and lay with its trunk propped a couple of feet off the ground. I looked, but I couldn't see anything, couldn't hear anything.

'So, where is he?' I asked Cola. 'I don't see him. I thought he was tearing around in here, you said.'

Cola had his mouth open to answer, when there was a sudden movement from ahead, a cracking and tearing of branches and brush, and a dark shadow the size of a large wheelbarrow burst from the shelter of the down beech trunk and charged straight at Cola and me. I turned to run, but whatever it was that was coming jerked up violently at the end of a chain or cable that trailed behind it. It struggled and plunged on its chain, snorting and foaming in its fury.

'See him now?' Cola asked me.

I saw him. I'd seen him before, though not since he'd grown to his size today. Herbie Murdock's prize boar weighed a little over seven hundred pounds. He was pitch black, pelted like a cross between a gorilla and a giant porcupine, armed with a pair of curved tusks as long as sickles, and ridged with a spine of bristles that belonged on top of the wall of a penitentiary: a true, authentic, natural-born Ozark Mountains Razorback Hog. He was the male at stud and star attraction of Pig Heaven, Herbie's petting farm on Route 10. Pig Heaven had the expected population: ponies, donkeys, calves, sheep, goats, bunnies, fowl; but Herbie particularly liked animals of the pig kind. He had tiny pigs from Asia, pretty pigs from Africa, normal pigs from the USA, Europe, and England – and he had the pig who faced us now, massive, menacing, and feral. Big John.

'See him now?' Cola asked.

'I see him,' I said.

'What are you going to do about him?'

'I'm thinking.'

'What's to think about, Sheriff?' Cola asked me. He laid his hand lightly on the butt of the pistol at his belt. 'Let me take care of this,' he said. 'I don't care. All that big son of a bitch is to me is free bacon.'

'No,' I said. 'Hold fast.'

'Too late, now, anyway, ain't it?' Cola asked. He was looking back along the way we had come through the woods. I could see two people advancing on us. One was Homer Patch, the Gilead constable, the other was Millie Pickens from the Valley Animal Rescue League. Homer was carrying a heavy folded-up net over his shoulder. Millie Pickens had an air rifle. The two of them made quite a pair. Homer was six-four or -five and framed large. Millie came up about to his elbow. She was a sparrow beside him. Homer and Millie looked like an old-time comedy team, but laughs were not what they were after, at least Millie wasn't, not that day. Though was she ever?

'This animal is suffering, Sheriff,' she told me when she and Homer had joined us. Big John strained against his chain, tore at the ground between us and him with his hooves, slashed the air with his yellow tusks, and kept up a series of grunts and snorts, trying to get at us.

'He's under extreme stress,' Millie Pickens said. 'Any second, his heart can stop, and he can die.'

'What do you suggest?'

'First, we need to free him from that chain. The chain, the restraint, is what's stressing him. We must turn him loose.'

'Go to it,' I told her. Cola snickered.

'We sedate him first, of course,' said Millie. She raised her air rifle.

'This is a tranquiliser gun,' she said.

'So's this,' said Cola, touching the butt of his forty-five. 'But with this one, the tranquil lasts a good deal longer.'

That wasn't what Millie wanted to hear. She turned to me.

'Sheriff?' she said.

'Okay, Ms. Pickens,' I said. 'Do your stuff.'

It took two of Millie's sedative darts and nearly an hour of waiting for them to work, but in time Big John was lying stretched full-length on his side, snoring placidly. Cola went down to his shop and came back with a bolt-cutter that he used to get the chain off the boar. Then Millie knelt at Big John's side and went over him. She put a stethoscope to his flank, raised his lip to examine his teeth, looked at his ears, looked at his hooves.

'Magnificent creature,' she said.

'Sure is,' I said. 'How long before he wakes up?'

'Hard to say.'

'Well, then, let's move it, Ms. Pickens. That okay with you?'

'Okay with me, Sheriff,' said Millie.

Deputy Treat and a couple of volunteer firefighters from Humber had showed up while we attended to Big John. Now Homer spread his net on the ground beside the giant boar, and together we rolled him into the net and hauled him in it through the woods to Cola's. There we used a chain fall to lift the unconscious boar into my truck. Big John would be lodged in the locked-down wing of the Valley Animal Rescue League's facility. Herbie Murdock or his caretaker at Pig Heaven would have to deal with him eventually. At the least, they would have to put up a better fence.

'I appreciate your help today, Sheriff,' said Millie Pickens. 'I mean your cooperation. I know what that Hitchcock would have done.'

'If Cola'd wanted to shoot Big John,' I told her, 'he'd have gone ahead and done it without bringing us in. He ain't that bad really.'

'Yes, he is, but thanks, in any case.'
'Okay, Ms. Pickens,' I said.
'Millie.'
'Okay, Millie,' I said. 'I guess we're about done for today.'
'Yes,' said Millie. Then, 'It's quite a job you've got, isn't it, Sheriff?'
'How do you mean?'
'Well, all the calls, the tasks. I mean, did you expect to spend this morning hauling a half-ton of anesthetised hog through the woods? In addition to the usual, the speeders, the wife-beaters, the break-ins? So many calls.'
'We're versatile in the sheriff's department, Millie,' I said. 'Why they pay us the big bucks.'

***

At Cola's, Big John had been taken away, and the party was breaking up.
Homer was in his truck, ready to go. I stopped him. Homer and I needed to talk; though Homer probably wouldn't have thought so. Too bad for Homer. I had two young runaways, and I had a mysterious campsite off in the woods. I wanted Homer to help me put them together. I was pretty sure he could. It was a question of making connections, and in the Valley, everything is connected to everything else.
'Homer?' I said. 'Can I have a minute?'
Homer gave me a careful look. 'I'm wanted home,' he said.
'Just a minute,' I said. 'I'll buy you a coffee.'

6
At Humphrey's

According to the old joke, there are cops without uniforms. There are cops without badges. There are cops without guns. But there are no cops without doughnuts.

Constable Homer Patch and I, cops after a fashion, were honouring the spirit of that joke in the back booth at Humphrey's. Humphrey put out a cinnamon doughnut that was worth the trip, provided the trip wasn't too long, which, to Humphrey's, it never was.

I gave Homer a chance to taste his coffee and take a bite of his doughnut. Then I went after him.

'You know those kids living in the woods by Truax's?' I asked Homer.

'Living where?' Homer asked.

'At Constance Truax's. Miz Truax? The teacher?'

'Oh, that Truax,' said Homer. 'What about her?'

'Nothing about her, Constable,' I said. 'About the kids in her woods.'

'What kids are those?'

I looked levelly at Homer. I drank my coffee.

'I don't know what you're talking about,' said Homer.

I took a bite of doughnut.

'Look, Lucian,' said Homer, 'I don't want to get anybody in trouble.'

'Nobody's in trouble,' I said. 'At least, not yet. The kids in the woods are a boy and a girl. The girl's from out of state. Her family's looking for her. The boy's Duncan March.'

Now it was Homer's turn to drink his coffee.

'I can help them,' I said. 'But I have to find them. Where are they?'

'What makes you think I know?'

'Constable?'

'Homer picked up his coffee cup, put it down again.

'Probably at Truax's,' he said. 'You missed them, or they ran off when they heard you coming.'

'The girl?' I asked him. 'Pammy? Pammy DeMorgan, is it?'

'Didn't get a last name,' said Homer. 'Pretty thing, don't talk that much. They turned up at my place Tuesday night. Could I take them in til tomorrow? Sure, I could. But I called Amy in California. She's Duncan's mom; she ought to know where he's gone to. Buster's whereabouts were unknown.'

'Per usual,' I said.

'Per usual,' said Homer.

Homer and Amy, Duncan's mother, were cousins. Homer had known Dunc all the boy's life. So for Duncan and Pamela, having run away from their school and hitchhiked to the valley, going to Homer's was a pretty obvious move. Where else were they going to go? Homer offered to put them up beyond that first night, too, but Duncan wouldn't. He knew a place, he said – evidently meaning the campsite at Truax's.

Homer reckoned he could go along with that, as long as he knew where the kids were, and as long as Amy knew. Like a lot of parents who have elected to put the continent between themselves and their children, Amy was a worrier. She was afraid Dunc had, or would be accused of having, kidnapped the girl, who, for all anybody knew, was underage.

'Plus,' said Homer, 'she was afraid Pammy might be you-know.'

'Is she?' I asked.

'She says she ain't. Says she can't be. Says they don't… they didn't… they won't… they haven't…'

'Hah,' I said. 'You been inside their little tent?'

'I have,' said Homer.

'One sleeping bag in there, right?'

'So what?' asked Homer.

'Come on, Constable,' I said.

'Come on, yourself, Sheriff,' said Homer. 'You think you might want to get your mind out of your shorts, there?'

'You're probably right,' I said. 'They're probably playing canasta or checkers all day and all night. That's probably it, like you say.'

'I don't care,' said Homer. 'She says she ain't you-know. Dunc says the same. I believe them.'

'How come?'

'I don't know,' said Homer.

I told Homer about the big-shot lawyer from New York who'd turned up, on the trail of the girl. I told about his even-bigger-shot boss, the girl's stepfather, Rex Lord. Homer said he knew about him.

'So, what's going on, really?' I asked Homer. 'Do they say? Did he cut her allowance, her stepfather? Does he make her pick up her room? Is he mean to her cat?'

Homer looked at me across the table.

'Does he beat her up?' I asked him.

'She don't say.'

'But you think he does?'

'Dunc thinks so,' said Homer. 'Dunc thinks he does worse.'

'Worse?'

Homer nodded.

'Okay,' I said. 'I hear you. So, what is it they're thinking?'

'They ain't thinking,' said Homer. 'Oh, I guess they're thinking they'll go hide out in Truax's woods for the rest of their lives, maybe build themselves a little cottage up there. You know: white trim, roses, white picket fence, plenty of vines, good cable package.'

'One sleeping bag,' I said.

'Can't get past that sleeping bag, can you, Sheriff?' Homer asked me.

'Instinct, constable,' I told him.

'Does your instinct tell you what to do about the two of them?'

'I was getting ready to ask you,' I told Homer.

'They think the girl's stepfather will figure out where they are and send people to bring her home. They want protection,' said Homer.

'I can't help them,' I said, 'or not a lot. They want a babysitter. I've got four deputies, two despatchers, and the part-time janitor. I've got a county that covers eight hundred square miles and has forty thousand people living in it. I can't detail personnel to bodyguard a couple of high school kids.'

'You could be on the case, though,' said Homer. 'You could talk to them. You could stop by their camp, keep an eye out for strangers around. You could do that.'

'I do that as it is,' I told him.

'My point, kind of, wasn't it?' Homer said.

'Okay,' I said. 'Yes, I can do that.'

We sat and drank our coffee and looked, for the thousandth time, over Humphrey's particular style of décor: framed newspaper front pages with big headlines out of the last – what? – seventy-five years? There they were, the whole parade: Pearl Harbour; The Bomb; JFK; RFK; Martin Luther King; Vietnam; the World Trade Centre. The news of a lifetime, of our lifetime, spread out in front of you. The news of our lifetime – and every last, single bit of it bad.

'What's the matter with him, Constable?' I asked Homer.

'Who?' Homer asked. 'The stepfather?'

'No, no,' I said. 'Humphrey, the owner here. What's the matter with Humphrey?'

'How do you mean? Is something the matter with him?'

'All this,' I said. 'All this war, death, destruction, calamity. Does Humphrey think it makes people hungry, or what?'

'You're depressed, ain't you?' Homer asked me. 'You better have another doughnut.'

That was Homer. A simple soul – or was he? He was a quiet old boy, didn't have a lot to say. But he had a left-handed sense of humour not everybody appreciated. Wingate didn't appreciate it, for one. Homer might have had the sheriff's job over me when Wingate retired, but he made Wingate – what? Uneasy. 'I don't know if that fellow's too smart for the job, or too dumb,' said Wingate, 'but I know he's one or the other. I don't need that. With you, I won't worry.'

Come to think of it, Wingate had a pretty left-handed sense of humour, himself. After all, your sense of humour, that's your mind, ain't it?

It's got to do with your brains. And, for brains, a good many in the valley thought Homer was lacking. They thought Homer was slow. Addison thought so. Clemmie thought so. I never thought so.

***

A day or so later, coming out of the bank branch in Cardiff Centre, I ran into the Father of the Bride. Addison was on his way down the steps. Was he putting in, or taking out? Putting in, I hoped. Clemmie and I won't be young forever. The county don't take good care of you. Addison's our retirement plan – or he'd damn well better be.

I stopped Addison and asked for a word. We leaned against the side of my truck in the spring sun, suddenly warm. The bank's daffodils were up, waving gaily in the new grass around the walkway. There were a couple of dozen of them, bright, thriving. It must be daffodils do well growing near money. Don't we all?

I told Addison about my talk with Homer, about the kids' hideout in the woods, about Amy's worries.

'She does well to worry,' said Addison. 'What is the kids' relationship, do you think?'

'Homer says they don't have one – not like you mean.'

Addison raised his eyebrows.

'Course,' I went on, 'at their camp, they do get by with one sleeping bag.'

'Ah,' said Addison. He sighed and shook his head.

'Star-crossed lovers,' he said. 'Crazy, thoughtless, burning for each other, the world well lost? They sound just like Romeo and Juliet, don't they?'

'I wouldn't know,' I said. 'Do they?'

'To the life,' said Addison. 'It's a beautiful thing, young love.' He paused. He shook his head. 'But, then,' he said, 'there's the downside, isn't there? I mean, look at what happened to Romeo and Juliet.'

7
What Happened to Romeo and Juliet

I needed to see these kids with my own eyes. I left my truck at Truax's. Ms. Truax was out front. I asked her if the campers were still in her woods.

'Oh, yes, I think so,' said Ms. Truax. 'At least, I hear the flute from time to time. I've gotten to like it. I hope you're not here to make trouble for anyone, Sheriff.'

'It's your property they're on, ma'am,' I told her. 'If you're content to have them up there, it's not for me to hassle them. I've got better things to do.'

'You say *they* now, as though you knew there was more than one person.' Ms. Truax was pretty sharp. 'Do you know that?'

'I'm told that,' I said.

'Wait,' said Ms. Truax, and she cocked her head to one side like a smart dog, listening. 'There it is, now,' she said. I could hear it, too, then: a tuneful whistling, almost like a child singing far off, faint but clear.

'Hear it?' Ms. Truax asked me.

'I do,' I said. 'I'll walk on up, since they're there.'

'Do you want me to come along?'

'No need,' I said. 'I know you're busy.'

Ms. Truax laughed. 'Busy?' she said. 'I'm far from busy, Sheriff. I've got nothing but time.'

That was about right. Constance Truax was retired from thirty years' teaching eighth grade in Jordan. She had observed, instructed, and controlled, or attempted to control, two generations of the valley's young. On her retirement, she had sold her place in the village and bought ten acres in Gilead, as far out in the woods as she could get, far from the road, far from business, far from neighbours – and far, very far, from eighth-graders.

Ms. Truax brought in a contractor to build her a simple log-cabin house, and she planted a big garden. From now on, for what time was left to her, she announced, she would stick to vegetables. With vegetables, you plant them out in the sun and water them, and they mostly do okay. With eighth-graders, Ms. Truax had found, that doesn't always happen – especially with the boys.

'Are you sure I hadn't better come with you?' she asked me.

'I've got it,' I said.

I went around the house, across the yard, and into the woods, past the hogweed, and on to the camp. There I found a young girl sitting cross-legged on the ground before the tent. She was blonde, slight. Carl Armentrout had called her seventeen. Close enough. She was playing on a flute, but when she saw me coming, she put it aside, quickly got to her feet, turned to the tent behind her, and said something I didn't catch. I went on to the camp.

'Pamela?' I asked the girl. 'Pammy? Pammy DeMorgan?'

The girl didn't reply, but the tent's door curtains parted, and young Duncan March came out and stood beside the girl. She came about to his collar bone. In his right hand he held a baseball bat. He nodded to me, civil enough, but not pretending he was glad to see me. 'Sheriff?' he said. To the girl he said, 'It's okay.'

I knew Duncan. Sure, I did, a little. I knew him to see around and say hello to, but no more, and, since he'd gone away to school, I probably hadn't seen him at all in a couple of years. Football agreed with him, I guess. He'd grown. He was taller than I was, six-one or -two, two hundred pounds. What they mean when they say *strapping*.

'How's Duncan?' I said. 'Haven't seen you in some time. How's school?'

'I just graduated,' said the boy.

'Good for you,' I said. 'You going on to college in the fall?'

'University of Michigan.'

'Michigan?' I said. 'Sounds like football.'

'That's right,' said Duncan. He turned to the girl. 'This is Pammy,' he said.

I nodded to the girl. 'You're classmates?' I asked.

The girl shook her head.

'Not classmates,' said Duncan. 'Pammy's a senior next year. What do you want, Sheriff? Are we doing something wrong here?'

'Well, I guess you might be trespassing,' I said. 'But the landowner don't seem to care, and if she don't, then neither do I. So, no, you ain't doing anything wrong. I just wanted to look in, see if everything's right. I like to know what's going on, you know? It's my job, you might say.'

'Everything's fine,' said Duncan. 'No problems.'

'Then what's the bat for?' I asked him.

Duncan and Pammy looked at each other.

'You worried about somebody?' I asked.

'No, nobody,' said Duncan. But Pammy was looking at me. I spoke to her. 'Your stepfather?' I asked her. The girl didn't answer, but Duncan spoke up.

'Her stepfather,' he said, 'and his friends, his men. He has, um, men.'

'I know,' I said. 'I met one of them.'

At that, both kids seemed to draw back a little.

'What else do you know, Sheriff?' Duncan asked me.

'Not much. Pamela's dad – step-dad, whatever he is – wants her back. He's looking for her. That's how I met this guy, a lawyer named Carl Armentrout. Works for Pammy's father. Know him?'

'No,' said Duncan. 'There are a lot of them, though. A lot of men.'

'There's Hector,' said Pammy.

'Who's Hector?' I asked her.

'Another creep of Rex's,' said the girl.

'So, this lawyer wants you to find us?' Duncan asked me.

'That's what he wants,' I said.

'What did you tell him?'

'I told him I'd look for you. Here I am.'

'And if you found us? What then, did you tell him?'

'I told him then we'd see.'

'But you're the sheriff, right?' Duncan pressed me. 'You're a cop.'

'Looks that way,' I said.

'So, that's it,' said Duncan. 'You're under orders. You're a sworn officer. If you find us, you have to turn Pam over. Or, you have to try. You work for her step-dad.' He raised the baseball bat and rested it on his shoulder, at the ready.

'No,' I said. 'I work for the county. Am I sworn? I guess I am, but I ain't sworn to Mr. Lord. I ain't sworn to his men. I do my job my way. Anybody don't like it can vote for somebody else next election.'

Pamela looked up at Duncan, and he bent to her so she could whisper in his ear. I couldn't hear her, but Duncan looked at me and said, 'Okay.' He laid the bat on the ground at his feet. 'So, we can stay here for now, right?'

'For now,' I said. 'What did you have in mind for later?'

'We're trying to get in touch with Pammy's mom,' said Duncan.

'Where's she?'

'On a boat.'

'A boat?'

'A big boat,' the girl said. 'A liner, like.'

'Suppose you reach her. What can she do?' I asked.

'She can send money,' said Pamela. 'She can get us out of here.'

'How long before you can talk to her?'

'Not long,' said Pamela. 'A couple of days. She'll be in Zurich at the end of the month. That's in Switzerland.'

'Well,' I said, 'then stay here. Do what you've been doing. Lie low. I'll be around. If there's trouble, whatever it is, call me. You got that? Trouble, you call me. You don't try to knock it out of the park with your bat, there. You understand?'

Duncan and Pammy nodded together.

'Don't worry,' I told Pammy. 'Your dad can't find you up here.'

'Yes, he can,' said Pammy.

Yes, he could.

***

Clemmie was putting on her nightgown. Three parts asleep, I lay in our bed and watched her.

'What happened to Romeo and Juliet?' I asked Clemmie.

'Who?'

'Romeo and Juliet.'

'You mean in the play? Why?'

'Something your dad said. "Look at what happened to Romeo and Juliet," he said. What did?'

'They died,' said Clemmie.

'You sure?' I asked her.

'Yep,' said Clemmie. She turned down the sheet and got into bed beside me.

'Died, huh?' I said. 'Too bad. I thought they got married.'

'Hah, hah,' said Clemmie. 'Very funny.'

Clemmie's assistant manager of the inn in Cardiff; plus, she's studying on the side to be a social worker in the schools. She needs the social work degree, she says, living with me. I ain't sure what she means by that. I'm easy to live with. Easiest fellow in the world. Ain't I?

'You sure they didn't get married?' I asked her.

'Only in real life,' said Clemmie. She took off her glasses and laid them on the nightstand. She reached over and patted my chest. She gave me a quick kiss on the ear. 'Sleep tight, Sheriff,' she said.

8
Heavy Lifters

Evenings, if Clemmie and I were at peace, I liked to stop at the inn on my way home. I'd have a beer and wait for Clemmie to finish her shift at the front desk. The inn had a nice, quiet little bar just off the entrance, out of the way of the dinner business. I'd read the newspaper or talk with Alan, the bartender, if he felt like visiting. There were four stools, and the bar had two booths. Today, the only customer, I took a stool at the end of the bar and ordered a draft. Alan brought it and went back down the bar. I was looking around to see if anybody had left a paper behind them, when Carl Armentrout got up on the stool beside me.

'Hello, Sheriff,' Armentrout said. 'What are you drinking?' He looked down the bar. Alan was at the sink washing glasses. He ignored us. Alan was a writer, when he wasn't working, so he was probably planning his new book. Do you plan a book? I wouldn't know. Armentrout rapped impatiently on the bar with his knuckles. Alan didn't respond. Armentrout rapped on the bar again.

'You want something to drink, Mr. Armentrout?' I asked him.

'Turkey rocks.'

'Then quit banging on the bar. That don't work here.'

'Oh, no?' said Armentrout. 'Well, then, maybe, if he doesn't get off his ass, he won't get a tip. I'll bet that works here.'

'That don't, either,' I said.

Alan came. He took Armentrout's order, and went to fill it.

Armentrout turned on his stool and looked at me.

'We're a little disappointed in you, Sheriff,' he said.

'Oh, gee,' I said. 'Why's that?'

'You know damned well,' said Armentrout. 'We expected to hear from you before now on Mr. Lord's stepdaughter. We've heard nothing.'

'Nothing to hear,' I told him. 'We're working on it.'

'Who is we?'

'Me, my deputies, the town constable. Fish and Wildlife.'

'You're searching the woods, the way you said you would?'

'Dawn to dusk. High and low. Every stick and stone.'

'How many people do you have on it, all told?'

'Well, four deputies. Constable Patch. Wardens. Say, ten.'

'Not enough,' said Armentrout.

'You wanted a quiet search,' I reminded him. '"Discreet," you said. You want more manpower? Easy: go to the Vermont State Police. File a missing persons report.'

'No report,' said Armentrout. 'No police.'

Alan brought Armentrout's whiskey. 'Bring the sheriff another beer,' said Armentrout.

'No, thanks,' I said 'I've got one going.'

'Bring him another,' said Armentrout. To me he said, 'Come on, Sheriff. Don't you want to have a drink with me?'

'Dying to,' I said. 'But I have to go.' Clemmie was standing in the doorway, ready to start for home. I got up from my barstool.

Armentrout turned and looked Clemmie over.

'I don't blame you, Sheriff,' he said. 'I'd go, too. She's the manager here, right?'

'Assistant manager.'

'And she's with you?'

'Sometimes. We're married.'

Armentrout kept his eyes on Clemmie, who stayed in the doorway and made no move to join us at the bar.

'You're a lucky man, Sheriff,' said Armentrout. 'She's very tasty. She can manage my hotel any time she likes.'

'Be careful what you wish for, Mr. Armentrout,' I said. I turned toward the door. 'I'll let you know about the kids, anything comes up. Where do I find you?'

'See that you do, Sheriff,' said Armentrout. 'As for me, I'm around. I'm close. You don't need to find me. I'll find you.'

'What a jerk,' said Clemmie.

'Carl Armentrout?' I said. 'You know him? Is he a guest here?'

'He is,' said Clemmie. 'I and everybody else wish he weren't. His name's not Carl Armentrout, though. At least, that's not the name he used to register. Bascom, Bassett – something like that. Not Armentrout.'

'How long's he been here?'

'Three days? Four? Too long for me. He's a bully and a pig. He comes on to the wait-staff. He pokes, he pinches, he pats. Yuck. He's even come onto me.'

'He has, has he?' I asked her.

'I bet that drives you wild with jealousy, doesn't it?'

'Wild,' I said.

'You don't look wild, though,' Clemmie said.

'I'm wild, sure, I am,' I said.

'Really?' said Clemmie. 'You look more kind of – I don't know – preoccupied.'

'That's it,' I said. 'You hit it. I'm preoccupied. I don't like working for people that can find me but I can't find them. I also don't like working for people with more than a couple of names. Those things get me preoccupied.'

***

Ms. Truax had the wind up. She called around noon. Something was going on in her woods, near her pot-less pot farm. She'd heard vehicles up there, and she'd heard voices, shouting. And she'd heard what she took for firecrackers or Fourth of July rockets. What were those kids up to? I didn't know, but I knew it wasn't the Fourth of July.

Deputy Treat was closest to Truax's, so I sent him on there while I took the long way, around the hill to the old logging road that went up to Duncan and Pammy's campsite from the south. You couldn't drive over that road in a cruiser, or even in my truck, but the sheriff's department owned an all-terrain vehicle with wheels on it like a moon-crawler. That rig could do everything but climb trees. I put it on my truck and set out.

When I got to the bottom of the log lane, where it came out on the town road, I saw somebody else had had the same idea, and pretty much the same equipment, as I had. Not good. The ground was heavily marked by big, deep tyre tracks. The tracks were going both ways, as far as I could tell. Whoever had driven in here had also driven out. Good.

I bumped and churned and roared my way up the trail, which was pretty steep in places. The campsite was farther into the woods from this direction than I'd recalled: most of half a mile from the town road.

Deputy Treat was waiting for me at the camp, or what was left of the camp. Somebody had gone over it pretty good. The tent itself was half-collapsed, and in several places it had been cut or slit up and down both sides. The food, clothing and other belongings that had been in it were scattered and kicked around. The camp looked like a bear had gone at it, whanging and flanging it and everything in it all over the lot, the way bears will do when they're after food. Treat and I stood and looked at the wreckage.

'They must have slashed the tent with a knife,' I said.

'They did more than that, Sheriff,' said Treat. He pointed to a dozen or so holes in the tent sides. Small holes. Bullet holes.

'This, too,' said Treat. He went into his pocket and took out a 9mm brass casing, then another. 'There's more,' he said. 'They shot it all to shit.'

'They sure did,' I said. 'They even shot up the girl's book of poems.' Lying on the tramped-down grass, Addison's friend W. B. Yeats had taken two rounds, through and through.

'Sheriff? Sheriff Wing?'

Deputy Treat and I turned. Duncan and Pamela were coming out of the woods toward us, Duncan leading, Pammy following close behind, carrying her flute.

'You two okay?' I asked.

Duncan nodded. He was a little winded. 'We heard them coming,' he said. 'We hid in the woods. They were shooting.'

'Like, guns,' said Pamela.

'How many?' I asked.

'Two. They were on a log skidder, one driving, one hanging on.'

'You know either of them?'

Duncan shook his head. He looked at Pamela. 'She does,' he said.

'Hector,' said Pamela.

'You talked about him before,' I said. 'He's one of your step-father's men?'

'No,' said Pammy. 'Hector's different. He's – I don't know – he's higher.'

'And he was here? He did this? You saw him?'

Pamela nodded. Duncan spoke up. 'What are we going to do, Sheriff? They know where we are. They'll be back, won't they?'

'You bet they will,' I said. 'So, now, pack up your stuff here the best way you can. Then go with the deputy. We'll get you situated for tonight, tomorrow. Then we'll see.'

My plan was to stash the kids at the sheriff's department for tonight. We had a holding cell, a lockup, converted from the second-grade classroom of the old schoolhouse. It wasn't Sing-Sing, but it was secure enough for now, and it was vacant. Our lockup was always vacant. The underwriters refused to let the room be used for the purpose our department had intended it to serve. In the valley, then, the insurance company did what no criminals, no drunks, no vagrants could: it closed the jail.

***

'They trashed the camp,' I told Addison later. 'They slashed the tent, they threw everything hither and yon. They had weapons. They shot the tent up. They even shot up the girl's book of poems.'

'You mean the Yeats?' Addison asked. 'They must be pretty bad, then, mustn't they? I mean, nobody doesn't like Yeats.'

'Tell that to Hector and them,' I said.

'Who's Hector?' Addison asked me.

'I don't know, for sure,' I said. 'A heavy lifter works for Rex Lord, I guess.'

'A heavy lifter?'

'You know,' I said. 'Muscle. A hard guy. A leg-breaker.'

'He sounds lovely,' said Addison. 'I told you there would be others coming along after your lawyer friend. Here they are. So, what happens now?'

'Well,' I said, 'the kids are at the department. They're okay there for now, but that's today, maybe tomorrow. They can't be there forever. They need a safe place to stay.'

'Ah,' said Addison.

'A place that's close, where we can watch them.'

'I see,' said Addison.

'A place where they can get to a phone, if they have to.'

'Exactly,' said Addison.

'You happen to know anybody might help them out?'

'Me?'

'Anybody who might have some room? Where those kids could go, just for a couple of nights, to be safe? Does anybody occur to you, at all?'

'Stop looking at me, Lucian,' said Addison.

9
Child of the Valley

Wingate wanted to take a ride up Beer Hill. He'd been lying awake nights, he said, trying to remember the old Metcalf place. Metcalfs' was one of the valley's historic sites. It was at Metcalfs' where, back in a simpler, more innocent age, the fellows down from Canada used to hide their bootleg booze in the barn loft under the rotten hay. When Mrs. Metcalf had a new shipment in, she would hoist Old Glory up the flagpole on top of the barn. The men of the valley would presently be seen straggling thirstily up Beer Hill. Mrs. Metcalf was a widow with three little kids. She couldn't run their farm alone. The way it must have looked to her, she could smuggle, or she could starve. And what of it? If people want a drink, they'll get one. Nobody thought any less of Eugenia Metcalf for helping them out. (Well, some did.) And, plus, it was all a long time ago, a very long time, even in Wingate's life.

Wingate didn't know the Metcalf place and its fame from the old Beer Hill days. He had been a little boy then. He had known it some years later, as an abandoned farm at the end of an abandoned road. He'd been up there a good deal in those later years, hunting. Wingate had been a wing shot in his prime, and the old pastures at Metcalfs', grown up to brush and saplings, were good cover for woodcock and partridge. So, now Wingate tried to remember: Was the barn across the road from the house, or same side? Did it have a cupola? Was the house two storeys or a storey-and-a-half? What about the silo? The sheep run? Wingate couldn't recall.

Therefore we went up Beer Hill to have a look. Of necessity, we went together. Wingate couldn't drive. He could barely walk. He lived in a room at the Steep Mountain House, the retirement home in Nineveh. There, Wingate kept in shape as best he could working out on Steep Mountain's exercise machines. He read mysteries. He watched TV. He played cards and chequers, but not too much. Less than you might expect. There was a reason why Wingate avoided the more sociable table games. He was a companionable fellow who enjoyed his friends; but he'd been sheriff in the valley for nearly forty years. That gave him a special point of view on his fellow inmates at Steep Mountain. 'Half the people with me in here,' Wingate said, 'I've had them in custody, one time or another. The other half I ought to have had – and they know it.'

'That's got to be awkward,' I said.

'Not for me,' said Wingate. 'But I don't know about some of them.'

Crippled up and creaky as he was, Wingate got where he had to get. That was thanks to a cast of volunteer drivers who, without much planning or organisation, showed up to transport Wingate. To the doctor, to the store, to the firehouse, to deer camp, to the Fourth of July parade, to the Veterans of Foreign Wars, the Little League game –

Wingate got there, assisted by the likes of Homer Patch, the Gilead constable; Cola Hitchcock, from the junkyard; me; and as many more helpers who were less regular but who reliably appeared when needed. Silently, invisibly, faithfully, Wingate was cared for. He was looked after. He was looked after, whether he liked it or not. In his deep old age, Wingate had become, once again, what he had been when young, what we had all of us been: another of the valley's common children.

Getting Wingate situated as he now was hadn't been easy. There were those in the valley who believed he had gone at least halfway around the bend. They had Wingate wrong. Wingate wasn't crazy, and he wasn't senile. But he was wicked, wicked stubborn. Being stubborn is a character trait, ain't it? And any character trait, if you ride it hard enough, you begin to look like you're nuts.

Nearing ninety, and fifteen years retired from being sheriff, Wingate lived on in the house where he'd been born, on Bible Hill in Ambrose. The place had primitive bare-wire-and-insulator electricity, a wood-burning kitchen range for heat, and fitful running water, but Wingate wouldn't move. His doctor, Dr. Bartlett, who was King Solomon in the valley, made a surprise visit to Wingate's place one day specifically to tell Wingate he couldn't go on living where he did. The time had come. He had to find a better place.

'No,' said Wingate.

The doctor told him about Steep Mountain House and other like places, places where Wingate could be comfortable, healthy, and safe, three things, the doctor assured him, that he most certainly was not where he was.

'No,' said Wingate.

'You'll like it there,' Dr. Bartlett told Wingate. 'They've got a good cook, their own van for day trips. They've got their own little clinic, their own lab. It's a top-notch place.'

'No,' said Wingate.

'You're a god damned old fool,' said Dr. Bartlett.

Wingate shrugged.

He'd be up on Bible Hill yet except that his chimney caught fire one winter midnight and burned his place to the ground around his ears. Wingate never would have made it out of the burning house alive, but Homer Patch, responding with the volunteer firefighters, went inside, through the smoke, through the scorching heat, up the stairs to the bedroom, picked up Wingate, and carried him out of the house on his back as the structure collapsed behind them.

Wingate spent the rest of that night under observation at the valley clinic. Dr. Bartlett found him there the next morning.

'Well?' Bartlett asked.

'Okay,' said Wingate.

***

Wingate was safely out of the old homestead, but the problem he put to his friends – to everybody in the valley – was by no means solved. It was made worse. It concerned mobility. Wingate was mobile. He kept his truck parked at Steep Mountain, in his designated space. The truck was paid off, it ran, and Wingate's licence was current. He saw no reason why he shouldn't use his own vehicle, especially as the alternative involved sitting around Steep Mountain playing penny poker with other residents, including those formerly apprehended by himself. To hell with that, said Wingate. A free-born, adult American, he hit the roads of the valley.

He also hit the trees, fences, houses and other obstacles of the valley. There was the problem. Wingate solitary, isolated, dwindling miserably away in his hovel on Bible Hill, was a danger to himself only. Wingate at the wheel was a danger to all. He didn't see well. He seemed not always aware of his surroundings, or of his speed. He drove halfway up the steps of the county courthouse. He tore the driver's side mirrors off every vehicle parked along Back Street in Cardiff. He drove off the road in Dead River and plunged a dozen feet down the bank and into the brook.

It was confidently expected Wingate would soon either kill himself, or demolish his truck, or, with any luck, both. Neither happened; Wingate and his rig were indestructible, immortal. The valley waited uneasily.

Then Wingate outdid himself. As it happened, I was there to see it. I was on my way to Brattleboro on Route 10 one morning when I realised the motorist up ahead of me was Wingate in his truck. Almost in the same second I recognised him, Wingate, no doubt having fallen asleep at the wheel, swerved sharply left, crossed the empty oncoming lane, ran onto the shoulder of the highway, oversteered right to correct, and accelerated. I mean, Wingate accelerated considerably. He roared back to the right lane, doing about eighty, crossed it, tore over the shoulder, hit the berm, went airborne headed for the woods, landed, flipped end-for-end, went airborne again, and came to a stop upside down and six feet off the ground, wedged between the trunks of a big double oak.

I followed Wingate, bumping across the open ground he had flown over, and approached the woods where he'd crashed. Others had stopped and were following on foot. I reached the oak with Wingate in his truck suspended from its twin trunks. I took hold of a trunk and pulled myself up to the driver's window. I looked fearfully into the cab of the truck. Wingate was sitting behind the wheel, held hanging by his seatbelt, looking thoughtful. He turned to me.

'Good morning, Sheriff,' Wingate said. 'So, what do you think?'

Wingate never agreed that this crash was the end of his career as a driver. He wasn't asked to agree. The valley took over, in the shape of Cola Hitchcock, who brought his wrecker to get Wingate's truck out of the tree and take it to his yard for salvage. As far as anybody knew, the truck hadn't been totalled – not even close – but Cola didn't wait to find that out for sure. He went to work, and in a day he had broken the rig down to nuts and bolts and candy wrappers. He then went to Steep Mountain, where he spotted Wingate a hundred-dollar bill.

'We square?' Cola asked Wingate.

'Well…' Wingate began.

'Good,' said Cola.

***

I stopped the truck and turned off the motor. We sat peering ahead down the green tunnel of the old road before us. We'd come almost two miles from the town highway. That was going to be about as far as we'd be going today, at least on wheels. In places, the old road was sunk eight or nine feet below the surrounding woods. It was more a trench than a road. Ahead of us, it pitched steeply down to a kind of rock fall, where tree trunks and boulders had dropped from the eroding earth above and blocked the way.

'End of the line,' I said.

To either side of the track, the forest crowded close, full of light, full of shadow, the branches of its million trees ticking and tapping at the sides of the truck, at its roof, as though a class of timid children wanted to be let in. You couldn't see more than twenty feet into the woods, they were that thick.

'This slide was here,' said Wingate. 'I'm pretty sure it was, maybe not as big as this. There's no road past this, or no real road, never was. Just a foot track. You came in from this end. You went up, and up, and Metcalfs' was on the level part.'

'Then we passed it,' I said.

'Couldn't have,' said Wingate. 'I've been looking.'

'So have I,' I said. 'You sure we're even on the right road? You sure we ain't lost?'

'We ain't lost,' said Wingate firmly. 'It's Metcalfs' that's lost.'

'You say so.'

'Look, Sheriff,' said Wingate. 'Metcalfs' wasn't some pissant four-tit operation, you know. It was a good, big farm. House, cow barn, horse barn, silo, shop, cribs, pens, yards, coops – I don't know what all else. It didn't just get lost in the woods. It couldn't have.'

'Where is it, then?' I asked Wingate.

'We'll find it,' said Wingate. 'Back her up.'

I told you he was stubborn. We went up and down the same road several more times that day. We got out of the truck and beat the bushes – or, rather, I beat them while Wingate supervised. We found nothing.

'I can't understand it,' said Wingate. 'I've been in here a hundred times.'

'How long ago was the last time, though,' I asked him.

Wingate looked around at the flickering green woodland, at the spare yellow sunlight, full of bright dust, that came down through the branches of the trees. He shook his head. 'Too long, it looks like, don't it?' he said

***

When I'd returned Wingate to Steep Mountain and was on my way home, Deputy Treat came on the radio, loud, clear, and unhappy. Beer Hill was located in a far corner of Gilead, a town that had radio and other communications service ranging from unreliable, down through substandard, to poor, to non-existent. Treat had been trying to reach me for several hours. He was in a state of excitement.

'Sheriff, where have you been?' Treat asked me.

'Bushwhacking,' I said.

'Me, too,' said the deputy. 'I've been bushwhacking, too, but I bet you had a better time than I did.'

'What's on your mind, Deputy?'

'Had a call from Herbie's new caretaker at Pig Heaven,' said the deputy.

'Uh-oh,' I said. 'Sounds like Big John. He out again?'

'Since sometime last night. Busted the fence right down.'

'That's the new, extra-strong fence?'

'Busted it right down.'

'Jesus Christ,' I said.

According to Deputy Treat, the caretaker at Pig Heaven had called our office when he'd discovered Big John, the monster boar, had broken out of his pen. Treat had gone up there and looked things over. He tried to reach me, couldn't. Then he began thinking for himself. He saw Big John had left a trail of destruction from his pen to the woods. He thought of George Murray, in Humber. Murray raised and trained bear dogs, long lean hunting hounds bred to scent, follow and hold black bears. These hounds were the dog equivalent of light-heavyweight prizefighters.

Murray loved to work them. He met the deputy at Pig Heaven with three dogs. They set out into the woods on the trail of Big John.

The trail wasn't long. The two men and three dogs had gone maybe a quarter of a mile following the smashed-down brush and torn-up earth that the hog had left behind when Big John himself came at them from the flank. He ripped one of the dogs with his tusks and knocked another flat to the ground. The third dog ran for his life. Murray went up one tree, and Deputy Treat went up another. Big John disappeared into the woods, wild, out of control, and looking for trouble. Not good.

'Murray's not happy, Sheriff,' the deputy told me. 'Says the dog that got cut up may never hunt again. Says the vet bills are on the department.'

'Jesus Christ,' I said, again. 'That's your report, is it, Deputy?'

'That's it.'

'Okay,' I said. 'I'll see you tomorrow. I'm going home. Over and out.'

So I finished that day tired, footsore, mosquito-bit, and with a highly dangerous beast at large in my backyard. No, not good. Not good at all.

10
The Hideaway

'Stop looking at me, Lucian,' said Addison. I was looking at him, all right.

Sure, I was. I knew Addison had room where our runaways could shelter. I knew it, and the rest of the valley knew it. The Free World knew it. Addison had room, not only in the big house in South Devon, where, for many years a bachelor, he rattled around like a peanut in a fifty-five-gallon drum, but also owing to his part in one of the valley's longest-running jokes: the Green Mountain Hideaway Motor Court.

It was Nelson Pettibone who built the Hideaway, sometime around 1960. In those days, you recall, what most Americans wanted out of life was to pile into the family Rambler and motor endlessly from one crummy tourist cabin to another. Nelson bought two acres where the Cardiff Road joins Route 10. He put up six cabins. There were two gas pumps and a gift shop. Nelson built a house for the office and living quarters for himself, Nadine, and the boys. With that, he figured, he was all set. What else did you need? You had a restaurant in the Cardiff Inn, at one end of the village. You had the diner, Humphrey's, at the other.

You had shopping and the movies in Brattleboro, half an hour down Route 10 in the Rambler. Nelson didn't see how the Hideaway could fail.

Over the next ten years, he found out.

He found out, first, that he had missed his time. In the Hideaway, he had constructed something the world didn't need: an up-to-date dinosaur. What most Americans wanted was no longer to drive the Rambler from tourist trap to tourist trap. What most Americans now wanted was to stay home and watch TV. The Hideaway was doomed. It was empty. It was silent. It was the idle ghost of the enterprise it had never been. In 1962, when the Vermont Department of Transportation straightened Route 10 so as to bypass Cardiff village and the crossroads, trade dried up altogether. Nelson reckoned he'd had enough. He and Nadine retired to Florida. They didn't sell the Hideaway; they hardly tried. What would have been the point? Who would have bought it? Their boys could hardly take the place on. Monroe was driving a taxi in Boston. Chauncey was somewhere in California, doing federal time. There would be no second generation of Pettibones at the Hideaway. Nelson and Nadine walked away.

The place stood empty for some years, a festering lesion of decay, disintegration and delinquent taxes. About 1970, the Town of Cardiff took ownership. A couple of years later, toward the end of a hard winter, the roof of one of the cabins collapsed under its snow-load, and the Cardiff Fire Department burned the structure as a training exercise in firefighting for its volunteers. Some in town suggested putting the remaining cabins and owner's quarters to the same use, but that never happened. Miraculously, in spite of its condition and its unpromising history, the Hideaway seemed to have found a buyer.

The buyer was Addison Jessup, my father-in-law. Addison wouldn't have been the first small-town lawyer to persuade himself he had the makings of a shrewd player in real estate. He went into partnership with Edouard and Ingrid DeJonge, the owners of the Cardiff Inn, and bought the Green Mountain Hideaway Motor Court from the town for Nelson Pettibone's unpaid taxes. The idea was to build an annex to the inn on the Hideaway's lot, solving at a stroke two acute problems: the hideous eyesore of the decomposing and partially burnt-out cabins, and the inn's being too small to operate profitably at its present capacity.

Addison and the DeJonges hired an architect, a landscape designer, interior designers, various consultants, and other members of those essential professions that combine to make the business of securing comfortable housing complicated, prolonged, and very, very costly. They got drawings, models, studies, slide presentations. They hired a custom builder from Connecticut. At last, they commenced site work. They began on May 1. It would have been better for the three of them – Mr. and Mrs. DeJonge and Addison – if they had joined hands on April 30 and jumped together off the highest steeple in the state.

Preparation of the Hideaway's lot was in its first hour when the excavators discovered that Nelson Pettibone, or whoever had originally designed the place, had subscribed to the Short Pipe school of sanitary engineering. Much of the site's soil was what Addison described as a semisolid faecal sludge. Not good. But worse was to come, when the underground tanks that had served Nelson's gas pumps came to light. The tanks were empty. They were empty because they had failed years, decades earlier and had leaked their contents into the ground. Work stopped. Phone calls were made. A field team from the state visited the site, inspected it, dug holes, went away. Weeks passed. Then a joint task force from the relevant agencies of the United States government arrived, inspected, dug more holes. They reported that the earth around the Hideaway was saturated with oil and gasoline to a depth of many feet. It was saturated, as well, with a soup of other pollutants nobody could account for, all perfectly lethal and some, Addison claimed, new to chemical science. There was one piece of good news for Addison and the De Jonges, however: as far as could be told, none of the substances contaminating the Hideaway's site was radioactive.

'Lucky for us,' said Addison. 'That might have been a real problem.'

Reached in Orlando by phone, Nelson Pettibone could shed no light on the condition of the Hideaway's soil. His memory was deteriorating with age, he feared. He suspected dementia. He did have some vague recall of dumping taking place on the site – never by him, needless to say – but the dates and other details were lost.

At this point, Mr. and Mrs. DeJonge came to Addison in desperation and asked that their partnership for developing the Hideaway lot be dissolved. Addison, of course, agreed. He was a gentleman, or he was nothing. He wasn't about to hold the DeJonges to an obligation that would have ruined them. But would the same obligation ruin him? Addison, along with the DeJonges, had lately learned a new word: *remediation*. What if the remediation of the Hideaway was his treat? What then?

'I'll be alright,' said Addison.

Would he? Really? He was now the sole owner of what amounted to a toxic bog or swamp. 'What are you going to do?' I asked him.

'I'm planning my next move,' said Addison. 'Drink?'

He hardly seemed worried, even when it became clear that digging up, cleaning or replacing, and sealing the Hideaway's poisoned earth so as to make the property safe and fit for use would involve costs beside which building Addison's and the DeJonges' fancy annex looked like a night at the YMCA.

Still, Addison remained calm. He was right to remain calm. Consider his profession. As a real estate developer, Addison had proved himself to be far out of his depth. As an attorney, however, he was comfortably, confidently in his element. Did the *EPA* and the *VPA* and the *USA* and the *ADA* and the rest insist on remediation? Very well. Addison would see them in court. Meantime, he would temporise. He would delay. He would kick the can of remediation down the road of jurisprudence. Life is long. The Law is longer.

***

It looked to me like we could stow our young fugitives, Pammy and Duncan, at the Hideaway. They'd be safe there, and we could keep an eye on them.

Addison wasn't keen. 'Do I really want Rex Lord's people knocking on my door?' he asked. 'His – what was it you called them – heavy lifters? They found the kids in

Truax's woods. They'll find them at the Hideaway. I don't need that.'

'If they find them, that's my problem,' I told him. 'Either way, they ain't going to knock on your door. They have no reason to. They won't connect you to the Hideaway. Not everybody knows the history, there, you know?'

'Are you sure?' asked Addison. 'I thought everybody did.'

'So, what's it going to be?' I asked him. 'You going to step up to this, or what?'

'Absolutely not,' said Addison. 'You saw what they did to the camp. They not only wrecked it, they shot it to pieces. They've got guns. I don't do well with guns. These people aren't the Garden Club, you know, Lucian. They're thugs, armed thugs. And you want me practically to invite them into my facility and turn them loose? Ridiculous. That's a valuable piece of property.'

'The hell it is,' I said. 'The Hideaway? The Hideaway's not a facility. It's a slum that's getting ready to fall down.'

'You say that because you can't see the potential,' said Addison. 'You have no entrepreneurial spirit. Stir your stumps, Lucian. Roll the dice. Do you want to be a bureaucrat all your life?'

'Who are you calling a bureaucrat?' I asked Addison.

'Sorry,' said Addison. 'But the point is, those people are not coming to the Hideaway. Consider the implications for my insurance, for one thing. Doesn't bear thinking about.'

'What's insurance got to do with this?' I asked him.

'Insurance has to do with everything, Lucian,' said Addison.

'What's Clemmie going to say when she hears you wouldn't cut those poor kids a break, threw them to Lord's goons, to that Armentrout. She don't like Armentrout any better than we do. At the inn, she told me, he's always grabbing her bottom.'

'No.'

'She told me so,' I said. (That wasn't exactly true, but I was playing my last card.)

'Hmmm,' said Addison. 'For how long would the kids have to be at the Hideaway?'

'Couple of days, at most. Maybe three, four.'

Addison poured out a short White Horse. He knocked it back. 'Oh, hell,' he said. 'Let them come. Who knows? Maybe it will work out. Maybe they'll burn down another cabin. Does either of them smoke?'

11
A Brace of Rocks

We moved the kids at night. Pamela rode with Deputy Treat in his cruiser, Duncan with me in my truck. I was a little worried about Dunc. In the day and night he and Pamela had stayed at the sheriff's department offices, it looked like he'd grown a brace of rocks, or at least he'd grown the mouth that goes with them. Not good. I wasn't worried about the mouth. I was worried about the rocks. I wanted a word with Duncan, and I wanted Pamela somewhere else while we spoke, so he wouldn't feel he had to show off for her.

'Where are we going?' Duncan asked me.

'We're going to the Hideaway,' I told him.

'The old motel? Why?'

'So you'll have a roof over your head, a door you can lock. So you're right in town, where there are people around, instead of out in the woods. So we can act, if the people who are after you think about making a move.'

'Let them make a move,' said Duncan. 'Fuck that, you know? Let them come ahead. Fuck if I care.'

This kid sounds like poor old Rhumba, back there, don't he? It's all *fuck this*, and *fuck that* these days, of course, especially with the youth. When did that start? If Miss Maitland at the District 1 school when I went there had heard that kind of language, that word in particular, from any of her kids, she would have taken him out to the playground and hung him from the jungle gym. But I guess poor Miss Maitland ran a little two-room school back in the hills. If you're at a high-class prep school in Massachusetts or Connecticut, taking Latin and so on, you can talk whatever way you want. Whatever way you fucking want, I mean.

'Take it easy, Son,' I told Dunc. 'The deputy and I have those people. They're our job. Your job's to keep your head down.'

'Fuck that,' said Dunc. 'Fuck that, and fuck them. Like I said, tell them to come the fuck on. I'll be ready for them.'

Uh-oh. 'What's that mean?' I asked him.

'It means I'll be ready,' said Duncan. 'My dad? At home? He's got guns. They're locked up, but I know where he keeps the key. He doesn't know I know, but I do. If those fuckers show up, I'll be ready. That's all.'

I pulled the truck onto the shoulder, took it out of gear, and turned in the driver's seat so I was facing Duncan March.

'Duncan,' I said. 'Listen to me. Don't even think about what you're thinking about. You are not going to freelance this thing. You're not up to it. These fellows are not the visiting lacrosse team from Saint So-and-So's Academy. They will run you over. They will chew you up and spit you out. Do you get that? Duncan?'

Duncan was silent.

'If you don't care what happens to you,' I said. 'Think about Pamela. They want Pamela. They have no interest in you unless you're in their way. So don't get there. The harder you make their job, the harder you make it for her, the more chance she gets hurt. You don't want that, right? Nobody does.'

'Nobody does,' said Duncan.

'So, you leave your dad's arsenal alone, you put your hands in your pockets, and you keep your feet on the floor. And you shut up. We clear?'

Duncan nodded.

***

Wingate used to say being sheriff in the valley had been easy money in his day. It was easy money because the people you were sheriff of were the old-time hill farmers, loggers, and mill hands, which meant they worked so hard just to get by and were so exhausted at the end of the day, they hadn't the energy to get into a lot of trouble.

It's still true, to an extent. The farmers and mill hands are gone, but we're still pretty law-abiding. There hasn't been a homicide in the valley in nearly ten years. Theft? Well, we get break-ins, but seldom of the high-value, high-loss kind. We get vandalism, mostly in the schools and cemeteries. We get domestic disputes and spouse abuse, but not that much, and there, too, things have changed: nowadays, we find women beating up on their menfolk as well as the other way around. Good to see, I guess: you have to stick up for equality, right?

I don't mean to say the sheriff gets to sit around all day and catch up on his reading. Not at all. We keep busy. I haven't said anything about the large automotive end of the job: crashes, speeders, driving under, and the like. We're busy enough, but for the most part we're busy, not about dark, deliberate, sure-enough crime, but about what Wingate called *foolishness*, the kind of misbehaviour that, nine times out of ten, if you go all the way down to the bottom of it you'll find those two benefactors of humanity everywhere, Mr. Jim Beam and Mr. Bud Weiser.

Easy money, then, sheriffing, the way Wingate said. Though, in the last few years? I don't know. Things ain't the same, and not only on the part of the wicked, the criminal, and the merely dumb. Our side is changing, too. Used to be, for law enforcement in the valley, you had the sheriff, and you had the wardens from Fish and Game and the State Police for extra push when needed. That was it, short of calling out the National Guard. Now, we've got cops of one kind and another swarming over the valley who we don't even know who they are. Hell, we don't always even know they're here.

For example, a couple of years ago, I opened the paper one morning to find a big story about the arrest of a fellow in the valley who'd been engaged in some kind of international securities fraud. His name was Aaron Nachtigal, and he worked out of his home, a vacation place in Gilead. The authorities had been after Nachtigal for years, I later learned. When they finally moved on him, they did it with agents and other personnel from the FBI, the IRS, the US Treasury, the Securities and Exchange Commission, the State Department, the US Post Office, and a couple of other offices whose names I forget. I'd never heard of Aaron Nachtigal. I'd never heard of some of the agencies that busted him. Nobody had taken the trouble to inform me of a major operation involving a couple of dozen people organised and executed in my own backyard.

I called Captain Dwight Farrabaugh at the State Police barracks in White River.

'You know about this Nachtigal business?' I asked Dwight.

'Pretty much,' said Dwight.

'*Pretty much?* What are you talking about?'

'I knew something was developing. I only learned the T and T yesterday.'

'The T and T?'

'That's time and target,' said Dwight.

'Time and target, huh?' I said. 'Listen to you. You sound like a TV show. You might have given me a call, don't you think?'

'Like I told you,' said Dwight, 'the operation was held very closely.'

'It's my county, Captain,' I said. 'So what if it's held closely? I should have had a call.'

'Come on, Lucian,' said Dwight. 'Open the door and step into the present, here. You aren't the Sheriff of Cochise anymore, you know. You aren't the Lone Ranger. You aren't even Rip Wingate. It's a team effort today. It's all about teamwork.'

'Tough to be on the team when nobody tells you there is a team or what it's doing,' I said.

'Not my call,' said Dwight.

'Okay,' I said. 'It is what it is, I guess.'

'I guess,' said Dwight. 'I've got to go now, Lucian.'

'Just for my curiosity, what was the guy guilty of, again? Mr. Nachtigal?'

'Bank fraud, or mail fraud, or some such.'

'But what, exactly?' I asked Dwight.

‘I’m damned if I know,’ said Dwight. ‘The kid from Treasury tried to explain it to me. Went right over my head.’

Now, mind you, as loud as I’d squawked at being kept in the dark while unseen powers made themselves busy in my valley, I wouldn’t have minded having that kind of manpower at hand for dealing with Carl Armentrout, his shadowy boss, and his heavy lifters. I would have been glad of it. But, why? What was my beef? So far, all I’d really seen in the way of misconduct had been the ransacking of Duncan and Pamela’s camp in the woods. Same thing happens a dozen times every Labor Day weekend – worse happens. As for Rex Lord? He wanted his stepdaughter back. Again, what was my beef – that he was rich enough to hire people to go out looking for her? No crime in being rich (except maybe in the gospel, I guess). The problem was mine. The problem was the same unseen powers that had combined to investigate and shut down Aaron Nachtigal. Only, this time, they weren’t on my side. That made me a little nervous. More than a little. It’s like dogs. Everybody likes dogs, and so do I, but I like to know where the dogs are at. Especially if they’re big dogs. Especially if they bite.

Clemmie says my trouble is, I can’t decide if I’m the valley’s sheriff, or its aunt.

***

Deputy Treat and Pamela were waiting for us inside one of the cabins at the Hideaway. They had stopped for pizzas, and soon after Duncan and I got there, the four of us were sitting on the floor of the cabin, dealing with a couple of large pies.

'This is like school,' Duncan said. 'This is like the dorm.'

'Except there's no weed,' Pamela said. She was enjoying herself.

'Maybe Hector will bring some,' said Duncan.

'If only he would,' said Pamela. 'I don't know any other way I could be, like, glad to see Hector.'

'Hold on,' said Deputy Treat. 'Just hold on. Am I in a den of dope fiends, here?'

'Could be,' I told him.

'Because, in that case,' the deputy went on, 'I might have to make an arrest.'

'You going to arrest me?' Duncan asked him.

'Not you,' said Treat. He turned to Pamela. 'You, maybe,' he said.

12
The Wager

The cabin at the Hideaway where we had parked Duncan and Pamela was four walls, a roof and a dirty window. No water, no electric. So, to keep the kids out of sight, Clemmie said they should come to us for their needfuls. One day shortly after they had moved to the Hideaway, then, I had a court date, so Deputy Treat drove Duncan and Pamela to our place. Clemmie was there with them. When I got home that evening, she looked as though she'd just peeked at her cards and found an ace up and two more in the hole.

'What?' I asked.

'Those kids,' Clemmie said. 'Duncan and Pamela. When we were talking the other day about Romeo and Juliet? The child lovers, dying for each other? Shakespeare? Romeo and Juliet?'

'What about them?'

'Boy, were we wrong, weren't we?'

'Were we?' I asked her.

'So wrong. Duncan and Pamela? Romeo and Juliet? I don't think so.'

'What do you mean?' I asked Clemmie. 'Why not? You've seen them.'

'Yes, I have. Have you? Open your eyes, Sheriff.'

'Open your own eyes,' I said. 'What about their tent? Their one sleeping bag?'

'A sleeping bag is a sleeping bag,' said Clemmie. 'But that's not the thing. The thing is, yes, I have seen them. They were here with Treat all afternoon. And, yes, there is a couple. But it's not Pamela and Duncan.'

'Who, then?'

'Pamela and your deputy.'

I laughed at that. 'Pamela and Deputy Treat?' I said. 'Not a chance.'

'Why not?'

'Treat ain't interested in Pamela. I mean, he ain't interested *at all*, not even a little bit. You know what I'm saying?'

'No, I don't know. Why not?'

'Why not? Do I have to draw you a picture, here? The deputy bats for the other team, is why not. He mounts from the block.'

'You're saying he's gay?'

'Bingo.'

'You're crazy,' said Clemmie. 'What makes you think he is?'

'All kinds of things. No wife in the picture anywhere, no girlfriend, lives alone, don't hang out at Humphrey's, or the inn. Comes in on his days off to catch up on paperwork, talks correct, always neat and tidy, never needs a haircut...'

'So, because he's single, not a slob, bathes, speaks English, and does his work, you think he must be gay. Is that about it?'

'Makes no difference to me, you understand,' I went on. 'We don't discriminate. We're Equal Opportunity, all the way. Anybody who can get out of bed in the morning and who'll work for the chicken shit I can afford to pay is okay with me. I don't care how he puts on his boots. Treat's a good deputy, a good man. But you ain't, ain't, ain't – are not going to see him riding off into the sunset with Pamela DeMorgan.'

'Want to bet?' Clemmie asked me.

'Sure,' I said. 'How much?'

'Fifty dollars?'

'Make it a hundred,' I said.

I knew I might have overplayed there. Clemmie's sharp. She don't often go wrong. But, the way I looked at it, more's at stake here than money. I was making a point. (Though what point, exactly?) And plus, the hundred's not lost. It's community property, ain't it?

'Okay,' I said to Clemmie. 'Say you're right. Say Deputy Treat's as straight as the centre line. So. What makes you think he and Pamela are an item?'

'They aren't one, yet,' said Clemmie. 'Or, they are but they don't know it. They'll find out. That's the way it works, sometimes.'

'The way what works?' I asked her.

'You know what,' Clemmie said.

***

I knew. That was the way it had been with Clemmie and me, to start. For a long time, we might as well have been going around in disguise, in dark glasses and false whiskers. We might as well have been wearing masks: we didn't know who we were. Then, one day, we did.

I was ahead of Clemmie in school. She says I robbed the cradle. It was more like I robbed the millpond. Clemmie was one of the little girls who went around like a gang of minnows, darting here and there, hard to follow, always together, quick, bright. You couldn't tell one of them from another; but, then, why would you want to? What were they? Little fish, was all.

I didn't get to know Clemmie as anything but a minnow until some years down the line, when I went to work as Wingate's new deputy. On patrol one day, I busted Clemmie for speeding on the River Road. I pulled her over and walked up to her little VW to process the stop. I asked her for her driver's licence, and she handed it to me. Without it in my hand, I wouldn't have known who Clemmie was that afternoon.

'Clementine Jessup,' I said. 'I know you. You sure you're old enough to drive?'

'Ha, ha,' said Clemmie.

'I almost didn't recognise you,' I told her. 'You know how fast you were going?'

'Lucian Wing,' said Clemmie. 'You aren't really going to give me a ticket, are you?'

'You bet,' I said.

Clemmie wasn't best pleased with that. She wasn't best pleased with me. 'You were a pretty nice guy in school,' she said. 'What happened?'

'Same thing happened to you,' I said. 'I graduated.'

At the time, I thought Clemmie was pretty good-looking, but not so as to make you fall down in a faint. She was smart, too, but so is everybody else, if you get to know them. And, then, there was the bookkeeping. With her driving her own car and her lawyer father in the state senate, or the state house, or whatever it was Addison was up to then, Clemmie looked like she'd be more than a little over my pay grade. Plus, at the time, she was the girlfriend of Loren Hinkley, her old schoolmate, who was going to Dartmouth.

For a year or so, I'm saying, Clemmie went her way, and I went mine. Nothing more to it. Nothing there.

Then, late one night when her father was in Montpelier and Clemmie was alone in the house in South Devon, she had a close call. She began to haemorrhage, couldn't get it to stop. She made it to the phone and dialled Emergency, then collapsed. I responded, got there the same time as the first medic, to find Clemmie on the kitchen floor in a big puddle of blood. She was passed out and white as a sheet of paper. More medics arrived, and we hustled her into the ambulance and burned the road to get her to the clinic in Cardiff. I rode with her in the ambulance. She made it to the clinic with about a teaspoonful of blood to spare.

Clemmie had had a miscarriage. Oops. She and Loren had been busy, it looked like. Good old Loren. And here we thought all you did at Dartmouth was hit the books and go to football games.

Clemmie was a patient in the clinic for most of a week, resting, trying to build herself back up. She felt okay, she said, but she was bored out of her mind. I wondered if that was better or worse than being bored out of her pants, the way she'd evidently been recently, but I didn't say anything. Anyway, it looked like Loren had moved on.

I found myself stopping by the clinic to visit Clemmie. I found myself doing that a good deal. I visited on the day of the night she'd been admitted, but she was asleep. I visited again the next day, and the next, and the next. And the next.

Wingate asked me, 'Are you still in the department, here, or what?'

''Course I'm still in the department,' I said.

'Oh, that's all right, then,' said Wingate. 'We wondered if maybe you'd retired.'

'Retired?'

'Thought maybe you'd taken up a medical career,' said Wingate.

One day I walked into Clemmie's room at the clinic to find her father, Addison, visiting. 'I'll come back another time,' I said, turning to leave, but, 'Not at all, Deputy Wing,' Addison said. 'Come right in.'

'Hello, Mr. Jessup,' I said.

'You two know each other?' Clemmie asked.

'We've met,' I said.

A couple of years earlier, late at night, on his way home from the bar at the inn, Addison had ridden the White Horse off the road and into the ditch. I'd found him peacefully asleep behind the wheel, woke him up, made sure he wasn't hurt, and driven him home. I'd held onto his car keys. I could have been sacked for what I did – or didn't do – that night; but I hadn't had any trouble from Addison before, and Wingate told us that in dealing with novice drunk drivers, it pays to go easy. With time and careful nurturing, those beginners can turn into loyal customers.

'I appreciate the way you handled that business, Deputy,' Addison said when I stopped at his house to give him back his keys. 'I might have been a trifle over-served last night.'

'Just a trifle,' I said.

So, for the week Clemmie was in the hospital, she and I saw each other every day. We didn't talk much on my visits. Clemmie lay in bed and watched the little TV fixed to the wall of her room, and I sat in a chair at her bedside and watched her watch it. There was plenty to watch, I found. The clinic had Clemmie in a thin hospital gown that had no sleeves and no back. I could see the blonde down on her arms, and if she sat up in the bed, I could see her shoulders and a piece of her long bare back below the collar of her gown. Sometimes, seeing all that, I'd have to excuse myself to walk up and down the corridor for fifteen minutes. Then I'd go back to the room.

Clemmie made good progress. The day before her discharge from the clinic, she put her hand on mine and left it there for about a five-count.

'I've enjoyed your visits,' Clemmie said.

'Me, too,' I said.

'Even though you don't talk much.'

'Sure, I do,' I said. ''Course I do.'

'No, you don't,' said Clemmie. 'You've been in every day for a week. I don't think you've said twenty words.'

'Sure, I have,' I said.

Clemmie shook her head. 'Not close to twenty,' she said.

'You want me to – what – count them for you?'

Clemmie smiled. 'You're kind of shy, really, aren't you?' she said.

'The hell I am,' I said.

'The hell you aren't,' said Clemmie. 'Never mind,' she went on. 'Either way, it's been really nice of you to come. You didn't have to do that, especially with me being a fallen woman, and all.'

'I don't mind,' I said. 'I like fallen women.'

'I bet you do,' said Clemmie.

'Always have,' I said.

'You don't say?'

'Can't stay away from them,' I said.

'Really?'

'Even though some of them talk too much.'

'Is that right?'

'That's right,' I said.

'Well, then…' said Clemmie.

When they let Clemmie go home, she was as good as new. Not me.

I wasn't as good as new. I was done for.

13
Omaha Beach

Distress call from the gas station on Route 10. When Evelyn, at the despatch desk, got the caller calmed down and halfway making sense, she buzzed me. It was Pamela. She was talking fast and breathing hard. She told of a knock on the door of her and Duncan's cabin at the Hideaway. A small, stout man with a British accent, very polite, wearing a porkpie hat, showed her a plastic badge on a chain around his neck and a clipboard in his hand, and advised he was the town of Cardiff's building code enforcement officer. There had been complaints about squatters at the cabins. Could he come in and have a look around?

Duncan let the man in. Not smart, you'll say, but the inspector was alone and unthreatening, and he made no trouble. He came in, peered here and there, shone a flashlight in the corners, got down on the floor and looked under the bed, and asked Duncan and Pamela how long they'd been at the Hideaway. Where were they from? Had they observed rats or other vermin on the premises? He made notes on his clipboard and got ready to leave. He'd have to file a report, he told Pamela and Duncan, but for the present they were okay. They should stay here, stay put for now. The man told them that twice: stay put.

Duncan was ready to take their visitor as offered. Not Pamela. She thought the man was wrong, wrong, wrong. She would not be appeased. Finally, she practically pushed Duncan out of the cabin, and the two of them ran through the woods to the highway and the gas station, where they called us.

When Pamela had finished, I got on the line with Dizzy Bernhardt, the manager of the gas station she had called from. The kids were still there. I asked Dizzy to lock them in the office. Then I got Deputy Treat on the radio. I asked him where he was. Clear down past Dead River. I had planned to have the deputy collect Pamela and Duncan at Dizzy's and take them back to the department for safekeeping while I went to the Hideaway. That meant a fifteen-mile hike for Treat, though, so I asked him if I'd better detail one of the other deputies.

'I'll be there in ten minutes,' said the deputy. 'Over and out.' Just before he ended the call, I could hear the screamer on his cruiser start up. Deputy Treat was on the case, all right, galloping off to the rescue – the rescue of Duncan, the rescue of Pamela. Was Clemmie right and I wrong about Treat's private, personal preferences as to this and that, and how they might relate to the present situation? No time to worry about it now.

I got into my truck and headed to the Hideaway with the throttle open. I pushed it, all right. I pushed it, because Cardiff is a good town. It's a pretty town. It has fields and farms and woodlands. It has rivers and streams. It has nice old houses, churches, and villages. It has, to near perfection, most of the things a town in these parts ought to have. But it does not have a building code enforcement officer.

At the Hideaway, I found the cabin empty, though it hadn't been for long. Somebody had worked it over in the manner of whoever trashed Duncan and Pamela's campsite at Ms. Truax's, but worse. The place was wrecked. The door had been ripped off its hinges, partly split, and knocked flat, as though by a battering ram. The window had been shattered. In the tiny bathroom somebody had smashed the commode and the sink and fired two rounds through the bathtub. They had also punched big ragged holes in the wallboard, maybe using Duncan's baseball bat, which lay in two pieces on the floor. Finally, the attackers had slit Duncan and Pamela's sleeping bag from end to end and scattered the down filling everywhere. The room looked like it had been in an earthquake, followed by a blizzard, followed by a tornado.

When I left the cabin to return to my truck, I found Carl Armentrout waiting for me in his town car, with his driver up front. Armentrout pressed a button to roll down his window.

'I'm glad I ran into you, Sheriff,' he said.

'Me, too,' I said. 'Awful glad.'

'I hoped you'd have some progress to report on my client's stepdaughter.'

'She's safe,' I said.

'She's safe,' Armentrout said. 'But safe, *where*? That's the question, isn't it? What can you tell me?'

'Let's you go first,' I said. 'You happen to know anything about all this?' I nodded at the ruined cabin.

Armentrout looked at the smashed door, the busted window, the downy feathers blowing gently out of the cabin and over the parking lot. He shrugged.

'Malicious mischief,' Armentrout said. 'Your young people up here don't have enough to do. You want to work on that, Sheriff. A Scout troop, Little League. That's what you need. The kids? They're bored, so they turn to vandalism. I've seen it before.'

'You don't know anything about this particular vandalism, though, I guess?'

Armentrout smiled. 'How would I?' he asked. 'Look, Sheriff, I bill a thousand dollars an hour. Get that? I don't lack for things to do. I don't have to go around shooting up motel rooms.'

'Who said anything about shooting?' I asked him. 'What about you?' I asked Armentrout's driver. 'You got any ideas, here? Any information?'

'Sorry, mate,' the driver said. 'Can't help you.'

Armentrout hit the button, and the window began to rise between us. 'I'm not sparring with you, here, Sheriff,' he said. 'Do your job. Find the girl. I'll be at the inn.'

Armentrout hit the button again. The window stopped. 'I'll be waiting for your call, Sheriff,' he said. 'Mr. Lord, my client, wants results from you. We agreed you'd lead the effort up here to find Pamela because you know the ground. It's your beat. I advise you to work it. If Mr. Lord chooses to put other assets on the case, here or elsewhere, well, that's his right. He may be tired of waiting. My client is a patient man…'

'You can see that by the way he did the room,' I said.

'…He's a patient man, but patience has an end.' Armentrout's window went up to the top, his driver put the big car in gear, and they rolled past me and onto Route 10.

As Armentrout's car left the Hideaway, Deputy Treat arrived from the other direction, with the hammer down. His cruiser fishtailed to a stop in front of the wrecked cabin, spitting gravel. The door flung open, and the deputy left the cruiser and trotted toward me. At his chest he carried one of our sheriff's department-issue police shotguns, ready for use.

'Slow down, there, Deputy,' I said. 'We're all secure here. Put up your scattergun.'

Treat halted. He held the shotgun at port-arms. He looked around.

'Where is she?' Treat asked.

***

Now, I've never claimed to be the smartest fellow in the room. For brains and education, I'm no better than the average, I guess. But I've held up my end. I've done my job. Mainly, I've done it, not by IQ, but by shutting up, by keeping my eyes open, and by remembering that most people's reasons for doing what they do, their motives, are pretty plain to see. Especially when they're up to no good, they generally go in a straight line.

So I have found, anyhow, and so I'd come to expect. Therefore, I didn't know quite what to make of Rex Lord, Armentrout and their heavy lifters. If they wanted to catch Pamela and Duncan, they had a funny way of going about it.

I put it to Wingate.

'They've shot up the kids' camp,' I said. 'They've wrecked their room. They've kept them on the run. They've scared them to death. Why? What kind of a way is that to do if they want to get ahold of the kids and turn the girl over to her stepfather? It don't make sense.'

'Sure, it does,' said Wingate. 'You've seen it. You've seen a rabbit being stalked by a fox. It sees the fox getting closer. What does it do? It ought to run like hell. Does it? No, it freezes. It's too terrified to run. "Scared to death," is right. That bunny freezes, and Mr. Fox –' here, Wingate suddenly snapped his fingers – 'Mr. Fox eats him right up. You've seen it. It works for the fox, it works for your friends.'

'They ain't my friends,' I said.

'I got that,' said Wingate. 'I was being humorous.'

***

I thought of Cola's. At his salvage yard, along with all his parts and pieces, he had a long-dead school bus: an engine-less, wheel-less, seat-less hulk stranded forever on the post-industrial mudflat that was Dead River Recovery. The mystery of the bus was that painted on its faded, rusting yellow sides was FORT WORTH PUBLIC SCHOOLS.

'That's Fort Worth, Texas?' Cola was asked.

'You know another Fort Worth?'

'What's a Texas bus doing up here?'

'Can't tell you,' said Cola. 'It was here when I came.'

I thought of that school bus at Cola's. Duncan and Pamela wouldn't have been the first to take shelter in its dank interior. The bus would do as well as the Hideaway for a refuge – it would do better. It would do better because Cola himself would be nearby. I'd given up on hiding the kids someplace and waiting for Armentrout's men to find them. Somehow, they needed to be under guard. I thought of Cola, and I thought of one of the few pieces of used-up machinery on his place that still worked.

I drove down to Dead River, found Cola at the yard. I told him about the runaway kids, about Pamela's billionaire stepfather, about the lawyer, Armentrout, with his limousine and his British chauffeur. I told him about the hunters of Duncan and Pamela, their wrecking the camp in the woods and the cabin at the Hideaway. I told Cola about my own lack of manpower, about my doubts that I could stop the pursuers.

'The way things are going now,' I told Cola, 'they'll get these kids, sooner or later. Probably sooner.'

'No, they won't,' said Cola.

Cola was armed and dangerous. In the woods behind his place the other day, he'd been ready to shoot Big John, the wild boar. Cola was armed and dangerous, and he was – what's the word? He was impulsive. There were plenty of people in the valley who thought Cola was crazy. I might have been one of them. But crazy or sane, Cola could be of use now, I thought. As part of his World War Two hobby, Cola kept up at Dead River Recovery a sideline in salvaged US military surplus. He had a couple of old Army Jeeps. He had an Army motorcycle with a sidecar. He had an LCVP amphibious assault craft. None of them ran, none had run since a least VE Day. No matter: Cola's collection also had a gem at its centre, a pearl of great price, in the form of a Browning Automatic Rifle, the .30 calibre light machinegun that armed our forces through at least three wars. Maybe the Jeeps, the LCVP, and the rest didn't run, but the BAR ran just fine.

'Where did you get a thing like that?' Cola was asked.
'Poker game,' said Cola.

***

Three or four days passed with Duncan and Pamela lying low in the bus at Cola's, under Cola's watchful eye. 'I don't see them,' said Cola. 'Hardly ever see either of them. They're in there alone, all day, all night. Not a sound out of them. Makes you wonder what they're doing.'

'Makes you wonder,' I said.

I knew Armentrout's forces would turn up soon enough; I didn't know exactly how. As it happened, when they showed, their cover wasn't well chosen. They stuck right out. They stuck out because they tried to pass as something Cola didn't see much of at Dead River Recovery: a paying customer.

Cola called me, said I'd better be at his place that night if I didn't want to miss the fun. He told me he'd had a visitor.

'Tall, skinny guy in a big Mercedes SUV,' said Cola. 'Wearing a blue-jean jacket. Looked like a – I don't know: a millionaire hay hand. Said he was looking for a starter to a seventy-five Pinto. Bullshit. This guy needs a Pinto's starter the same way I need a starter for my Gulfstream. He wanted to look around, see the office, see the shop. So I took him through the place, looking for that starter. I saw the girl, Pammy, peek out the window of the bus once, but the guy's back was turned. He wasn't interested in the bus, or if he was, he didn't let on. By and by, he'd seen enough. He got on his way. Believe it or not, we did find the Pinto starter. He gave me fifty bucks for it. Worth five. He'll be back. I hope he hurries. I'm bored.'

Cola wasn't bored for long. That same night, the opposition moved. Cola and I were waiting for them. You could say Armentrout's men walked into Cola's trap. You could also say Cola went over the top and nearly got everybody killed. Either way, the result was pretty much unlubricated hell.

I got to Cola's about eight. He had us set up in the cupola of an old barn on the junkyard property. Cola had rigged a couple of floodlights up there, and he'd lugged the heavy BAR up the stairs to the cupola and rested it on the railing, ready to go.

The opposition turned up around ten. In the moonlight, we couldn't be certain, but we thought two men in two vehicles, one of them the Mercedes SUV of the tall fellow who bought the new starter. They fanned out across the foreyard of Dead River Recovery and began to advance. One was armed with a shotgun, the other might have had a pistol; it was hard to see.

When Cola judged the pair were as close as he wanted them, he hit the switch for the lights and cut loose with the BAR.

For a couple of moments, everything went up at once. The deafening, clattering roar of the BAR, the clanging of the rounds hitting Cola's yard full of scrap metal, the whizz of the ricochets, screams from Pamela in the school bus, yells from the attackers, the sound of their weapons as they blindly, wildly returned Cola's fire, the glaring electric lights – you didn't know if you were in the valley or on Omaha Beach.

Yet, with it all, not much damage was done. Cola admitted later he'd been over-gunned. The BAR, firing on full-automatic, quickly escaped his control. Cola isn't a big man. He's wiry, but slight. Blazing away up in our guard post atop the barn, he was like a little boy trying to hang onto a fire hose.

'The son of a bitch got away from me,' said Cola.

Still, the trap had been sprung. The raiders had fled into the night.

I'll admit that when Cola opened up with his BAR, I had hit the deck, covered my head with my hands, and fast-crawled on my elbows and belly toward the stairs to the cupola; but the firing lasted less than a minute, and when it had stopped, I climbed back up the stairs, to find Cola in the cupola in a high good humour. He thought he might have winged one of the attackers.

'Anyway,' he said, 'we got their attention tonight. We showed them tonight. We jacked the game up on them a notch or two tonight. Didn't we? Didn't we? Hot damn, Lucian! This beats the hell out of selling scrap metal, don't it?'

Cola was tickled. He was having a good day. As for me, I was asking myself, *Okay, where to now?*

14
Places in the Woods

Carlotta Campbell DeMorgan Lord Campbell came into the valley like a travelling show. I had expected her to wire money so Pamela and Duncan could get well away. That wouldn't do for Carlotta, I found.

Carlotta loved to make an entrance. Hired car, uniformed driver – every bit as posh as Carl Armentrout's – half a dozen suitcases and bags. She had everything but the trained monkeys. Though, I guess she had them, too, didn't she? In the form of us. 'Good old Lottie,' said Addison.

Since parting from Rex Lord, she had been living discontentedly in London, with the Arabs, the Indians, the Persians, the Russians, the Chinese. Carlotta was glad to leave, she said. London had changed. 'My dear, you should see Kensington. I mean, you might as well be in the fucking *souk*.'

Carlotta had flown into New York and been collected by a private livery service for the drive to the valley. There, she had gone to Addison's. They had remained friends over the years, though they seldom met. It had been Addison who had gotten through to Carlotta, then vacationing in Switzerland, with the news of Pamela's going missing.

'I was in Gstaad,' said Carlotta. 'Of course, I dropped everything and flew to my little girl. I mean, flew. I mean, business class. I mean, steerage. But really, darling,' she turned to her daughter, 'look at you. You're a wraith.'

'Probably the food at St. Bart's,' said Addison. 'We'll fatten her up.'

'She's an absolute wraith,' said Carlotta.

Pamela rolled her eyes. 'I'm fine,' she said. You got the idea she and her mother weren't best friends.

Addison turned to Carlotta. 'You were in Gstaad by yourself?' he asked her.

'No.'

Addison raised an eyebrow. He waited.

'Rex was with me,' said Carlotta.

'Rex?' Addison looked at Carlotta, then at Pamela, then at me, then back at Carlotta. 'Really?' he asked. 'How does that happen?'

'Rex and I are reassessing,' said Carlotta.

'Reassessing?' Addison asked her. 'After everything? After this business up here, now? After he's been threatening your daughter, chasing her, hunting her? After that, you're *reassessing*?'

Carlotta waved him off with a flick of her elegant wrist. 'Oh, please, darling,' she said. 'Please. We're not children. I know Rex perfectly well. I ought to. I was married to him for seven miserable years. I mean, we all know what Rex is. He's a criminal. He's a monster. But, at the end of the day, he's so fucking *rich*. Isn't he?' (Carlotta sounded like Duncan trying to show tough. Our old teacher would have hung them both from the same bar.)

***

Holiday's was Homer's idea. It wasn't mine. I'd run out of ideas. One way and another, we'd been flushed out of all the best holes, and, after the firefight at Cola's, nobody was too eager to try the Omaha Beach route again. So Homer said why not take the kids out to Holiday's, stick them in the sugarhouse there? That didn't seem to me like a big improvement over what we'd been doing, but nobody had a better plan. Holiday's sugarhouse it was, then.

Holiday's place was in the Mount Nebo district of the town of Jordan. In our grandparents' time (well our great-grandparents') Holiday's had been like everyplace else in the valley: it had been a struggling little farm. But the last struggling, farming Holiday had long since gone down the road, and his successors had sold off most of the land. The farmhouse had become a summer place for a party of concert musicians from Boston, all women, mostly large women, who got up to God knew what at Holiday's, when they weren't sawing and squawking away on their violins or cellos or whatever the hell. Nobody knew quite what to make of those musical ladies, but they kept to themselves and caused no trouble, so they were left alone. Homer was their caretaker.

Holiday's, then, amounted to the farmhouse, set near the road, and the sugarhouse, which stood off on a little knoll. When the owners weren't around, the sugarhouse became a popular party spot. The young of the community found their way there to drink beer, smoke dope, and otherwise misbehave. Over the years, our office had gotten to know the sugarhouse far too well from rousting half the senior class of Cardiff High out of there one time or another and sending them home. Holiday's sugarhouse was a nuisance, was what it was.

With that in mind, I once quietly suggested to Homer that he and I take a half-gallon of kerosene up to Holiday's some dark night and do what needed to be done by the sugarhouse. I found Homer reluctant. It turned out he himself liked to get up to the sugarhouse during deer season. He'd stay in it for a couple of days, build a campfire in the old brick arch for the evaporator, live on beans and hash out of cans. Maybe a little whiskey. No venison: Homer claimed he'd yet to so much as see a deer at Holiday's. But, still, he wouldn't have it gone. Okay, okay.

***

Homer came along when Pamela and Duncan moved to Holiday's.

'You don't have to,' I said. 'We've got it.'

'I better come,' Homer said. 'I've got the key.'

'There's a key?'

'Well, not exactly,' said Homer. 'But I'd better come along all the same. I said I'd keep an eye on the place.'

'Said to who?' I asked him.

'The musical gals,' said Homer. 'I try to help them out when I can.'

Homer and Duncan rode to Holiday's together, with Pamela and me following close. Truth is, I was glad to have Homer along. Armentrout's heavy lifters had no way that I knew of to place us at Holiday's; but, then, they'd had no way to place us at the Hideaway, at Cola's – and they had. Those fellows knew a lot, it seemed. I couldn't be sure who might be waiting for us at Holiday's, or be turning up. Therefore, Homer was welcome enough, to me. So Pamela climbed into the truck beside me, with her duffel and the case for her flute.

'Where are we going?' Pamela asked me as we set out after Homer and Duncan.

'A place in the woods we know. Holiday's.'

'Like, *again*?' asked Pamela. 'Another place in the woods?'

'Places in the woods is about all I've got,' I told her.

'Is it a safe place?'

'You bet,' I said.

'Because, up to now, you know? Your places? The tent? The motel? The bus? They were all right, I mean, but they weren't exactly, like, safe, were they?'

'No,' I said.

'I hope this one is,' said Pamela.

'Either way, your mother's here now,' I said. 'You're all set, then, right? You'll be going with her. You'll be getting out of here.'

'I'll be getting out of here, but not with her.'

'No? Weren't you glad to see your mom?'

'I was glad to see her Gold Card,' said Pammy. 'Other than that, not so much. Carlotta's not exactly the Mother of the Year, Sheriff. We don't see a lot of each other, you know?'

'So where are you going to go?'

'School friends. They'll let me stay till classes start in a couple of weeks. My father's in Mexico. I could go to him. I'll be fine. I'll be fine anywhere but where Rex is.'

'And that's another thing,' I said. 'What about Lord? What's he done to you?'

'We won't talk about that, Sheriff,' said Pammy.

'There are things you can do, you know,' I told her. 'I don't mean me, or here. There are steps you can take, about Lord, I don't care how rich he is.'

But Pammy shook her head.

'Okay,' I said.

'What about Dunc?'

'What about him?'

'You and Dunc are together, right? Will he be going with you?'

'No. Duncan's a good guy. We're friends. But we're not *together*, all right? Not the way you mean.'

'What way do I mean?'

'Besides,' Pammy went on. 'This is Duncan's home. He belongs with you, in this place. Not me. I'm all done up here.'

'Okay,' I said again. 'I guess you know what you're doing – as much as most people do. Good luck. And don't worry about what's-his-name, Hector, and his friend. You're safe where we're going, for now. Don't worry.'

'Oh, I'm not worried, Sheriff,' said Pamela. 'Not worried at all. You know?'

Uh-oh. This is starting to sound like Duncan again, I thought – Duncan with his vocabulary cleaned up. I faced Pamela. She sat with her hands in her lap, looking serenely ahead.

'I'm not sure I do know,' I said. 'What do you mean, you're not worried, now?'

Pamela smiled and opened her instrument case. In it was, no flute, but an Army .45 pistol.

'Jesus Christ!' I said. 'Where did you get that? Wait a minute: is that Cola Hitchcock's forty-five? It is, ain't it?'

'Mr. Hitchcock gave it to me when we were in his old bus,' said Pamela. 'He said I could use it if I had to.'

'He did, huh?' I said. 'Well, that's just great, ain't it? Have you ever even seen a gun close up? Do you even know how to fire it?'

'Mr. Hitchcock says there's nothing to it. He showed me,' said Pamela. She took the pistol from the case. 'You pull this little piece back…' she said, and she began to cock the hammer.

'*No*,' I said. 'Stop. Stop right there.' I reached to her and put my hand over hers as it held the weapon. 'Just stop, okay?' I said again. I let the hammer of the forty-five safely down. 'You'd better give this to me for now,' I said. 'I'll get it back to Cola.'

But Pamela was having none of that. She shook her head. 'I don't think so,' she said.

'Miz DeMorgan,' I began. 'Pamela. Listen to me. I've been doing this job a good many years. I've seen a lot of screwed-up situations. Now, I'll admit to you, I ain't sure any of them was screwed up quite as bad as this here, but some came close, if you can believe it. My point is, I never yet saw a screwed-up situation that was made less screwed-up by a gun.'

Pamela shook her head again. She held tight onto the Colt, but she did put it back in the flute case, which she closed and latched. I shut up, and we drove on to Holiday's. It looked like Duncan wasn't the only one growing a set of rocks. Pamela was doing the same, and, between Duncan's new rocks, lodged mainly in his mouth, and Pammy's, assisted by Cola's forty-five, I thought I'd back Pamela. After all, Duncan talked about guns, guns belonging to other people, like his father, Buster. Pamela wasn't just talking. In the gun department, she was prepared, equipped and open for business. So now we had an armed highschool girl helping out, along with the rest of the team. Not good.

***

At Holiday's, Homer and the two kids and I set to work sweeping out the beer cans, pizza boxes, cigarette butts, and used condoms. We'd brought blankets and supplies for Pamela and Duncan. Pamela's mother would soon be getting Pamela to safety permanently, getting her out of the valley – clear out of the country if she wanted. Another day or two should see us through.

When I left them, Homer stayed on with the kids in the sugarhouse. Again, he volunteered for that. Homer wasn't any part of the sheriff's office: I couldn't have ordered him to baby-sit Pamela and Duncan. I couldn't have detailed any of my deputies to get into what was, as far as anyone knew, somebody's private business. Homer stepped up.

'I'll stay along,' said Homer. 'What else have I got to do?'

'I appreciate it,' I told him. 'I can fix you up with a weapon of some kind, if you like.'

'No need,' said Homer.

'What are you going to do if the other side checks in?' I asked Homer.

'I'll reason with them,' said Homer. Homer's a calm man. He don't let much get him going. I knew better than to force the point with him now. Like Wingate, like other calm fellows, Homer's also stubborn as a stump. He'd walk away if pushed, and I needed his help. He remained at Holiday's with Pamela and Duncan, unarmed. Homer would keep the kids out of trouble and entertained, no doubt by telling them how things were in the old days, along with other matters known to be keenly interesting to the young.

For example, Homer might tell them about the time when the musical women at Holiday's had called him up there as town constable because they feared some vagrant or fugitive was living in the sugarhouse. This same sugarhouse. Homer wasn't constable in Mount Nebo at the time. Mount Nebo didn't have a constable. The women had no business bringing Homer into their situation. But he went up there anyway, to help them, and because he was pretty sure he knew what was going on. He was pretty sure it was Hugh Calhoun, the town juvenile delinquent, who had moved into Holiday's sugarhouse, his father having kicked him out again. Hugh had been in there a week when the women came up from Boston to commence the summer's music-making. They had found signs of Hugh's occupying the sugarhouse, though Hugh himself was away just then. The women wanted Homer to arrest the trespasser. Homer didn't tell them he wasn't the right constable for them. He said he'd look into the matter.

Homer got right to work. He waited for Hugh on the road to Mount Nebo where you turn to go up to Holiday's. When Hugh came along, Homer told him it was time to move on. The two of them had a full and frank exchange of views. And, it's true, Homer leaned on Hugh a little, but only a little. Hugh moved on.

That was all there was to the business for Homer, and for the musical women, but not for Hugh. Homer had suggested he consider a change of scene. Soon after, therefore, Hugh went into the Marine Corps. When he came out, he was a different Hugh. Now he manages an auto parts store in Brattleboro. He's a deacon in the Valley Chapel. They take the Lord pretty seriously over there. Hugh will tell you it was the Lord who got him straightened out – the Lord, with Homer's help. Hugh was going to Hell in a top hat, he admits, when the Lord chose Homer to be His Instrument for the salvation of Hugh.

'I guess that makes you a pretty important fellow, don't it?' Homer was asked.

'His will be done,' said Homer.

***

Clemmie took off her glasses and laid them on her night table. She looked down at me lying beside her, and gave me her left elbow gently in the ribs.

'You awake?' she asked.

'I am, now,' I said.

'I've been thinking.'

'Oh, God,' I said.

'You know something I just this minute figured out?' Clemmie asked.

'Mmmm?'

'All this time?' said Clemmie. 'Everybody's been so worried on account of Rex Lord? Everybody's been so certain he's the villain; he's the one up in the attic, pulling the strings?'

'Mmmm?'

'It's not so,' said Clemmie. 'Lord's not running this thing. He never was.'

'Who is, then?'

'My ass-grabbing guest at the inn: Carl Armentrout.'

'And how do you get to that,' I asked Clemmie.

'From Armentrout's keeping everything so small and under cover,' Clemmie said. 'No police, no publicity, just you: a woodchuck with a badge.'

'Hey, thanks,' I said.

‘All that secrecy,’ Clemmie went on. ‘That’s not from Lord. That’s not his interest. He’d call in the cavalry if finding Pamela was what he was after. I bet he doesn’t even know she’s missing. Armentrout’s the one who needs to keep the whole thing close – until he finds Pamela and cashes her in.’

‘Wrong,’ I said. ‘You make too big a deal out of Armentrout. He’s an asshole, sure, but he’s a hired hand. Lord pulls the trigger, and Armentrout goes bang. He’s a tool. That’s all he is.’

‘That’s all he wants you to believe he is,’ said Clemmie. ‘In fact, Armentrout’s not number two, he’s number one. Always has been. That’s the trick: he’s not following orders from Lord or anybody else. He’s working his own end, here.’

‘What end is that, Nancy Drew?’

Clemmie shot me a look, but she wasn’t to be drawn.

‘The end of getting around you, finding Pammy, holding her, kicking Duncan free, and then going to Lord and telling him if Carlotta wants to see her daughter again, he needs to pay up.’

‘You mean like a ransom?’ I asked Clemmie.

‘Not *like* a ransom,’ she said. ‘A ransom. What do you think?’

‘I think you watch too much TV.’

‘Oh, I do? Why?’

‘You make things complicated, that ain’t. We’ve got no reason to believe Armentrout ain’t what he says he is. And plus, we’ve got Pamela and Carlotta telling us what kind of fellow Lord is.’

‘Don’t give me Carlotta,’ said Clemmie with a sniff.

‘What’s the matter with her?’

'What's the matter with Carlotta?' Clemmie asked. 'Let me see if I can think. Okay, she's a total fraud, for one thing. She likes to play the high society hostess, la-di-dah, darling – blah, blah, blah. Daddy says her father was a cop in the Bronx.'

'What's wrong with being a cop?'

'The Bronx is part of New York City,' Clemmie said.

'I know what the Bronx is,' I said. 'What's wrong with being a cop?'

I guess Clemmie didn't feel like climbing into that particular ring right then. She went ahead.

'Daddy also says Carlotta dumped DeMorgan, her British husband, not only because of his brains or lack of them, but because she found she'd overestimated his bank balance. That's why she's talking about making it up with Rex Lord. She's a what-do-you-call-it? A gold digger. Good luck to her.'

'What's that got to do with whether Armentrout is or ain't working on his own hook or for Lord?'

'Nothing,' said Clemmie. 'I just thought I'd mention it.' She reached to turn off the light.

'Thanks.'

'Thought you should know what kind of people you're dealing with.'

'Thanks a lot,' I said.

Clemmie slipped down in the bed and turned beside me, getting herself comfortable. She patted my chest under the covers. She gave me my goodnight kiss on the ear.

'Sleep tight, Sheriff,' said Clemmie.

15
The De-Escalation of Buster

When I got to work the next day and found Buster March's big rig parked, as much of it as would fit, in the lot at the sheriff's department, I thought, Uh-oh. Not good. Our little drama of Pamela and Duncan, Armentrout and his helpers had suddenly added a character I could have done far better without.

No help for it. Buster had been waiting for me. When I left my truck, he stepped down from the cab of his semi-trailer, advanced on me, and proceeded to climb up my chest.

'Hello, Buster,' I said. 'When did you get in?'

'Couple of hours ago,' said Buster. 'What the fuck is going on?'

'You didn't have to wait out here,' I told him. 'You ought to gone on into the office. The despatch could have bought you a cup of coffee, at least.'

'I asked you a question, Sheriff,' Buster said. 'What's going on? Where's my boy?'

'Come on,' I said, and led the way into the office, with Buster spitting, hissing and sizzling behind me like a walking grease fire.

Randolph March, Buster, was a long-trip trucker with St. Johnsbury. Out of any given month, he was home no more than a week or so, and when he was out of town, he was apt to be a long way out: New York, Florida, Texas – even Alaska, even Mexico a couple of times.

Whether it was because driving truck gave him a bad back, or indigestion, or piles, or some other painful condition, Buster was not a happy fellow. In fact, he was a mean, snarling, bad-tempered son of a bitch. He was also the father of Duncan March. That was bad luck for Duncan, and for his friends, teachers, team mates, coaches, and anybody else he had to do with. Buster's wife, Duncan's mother, Amy, had long since divorced him, remarried, and moved to California. Buster farmed Duncan out to different aunts, uncles and cousins when he was on the road. The boy lived in spare rooms and attics, on sofas and in sleeping bags up and down the valley. It wasn't for nothing that Deputy Treat had called Duncan the orphan. Addison called him Huckleberry Finn, after the kid in the book.

Being virtually homeless was the easy part for Duncan, though, probably. When he was little, Buster whipped and beat him freely. The boy was gaudy with bruises, bumps and welts. Duncan ought to have been taken out of his father's house and turned over to the state's child welfare services, and Buster ought to have found himself up in front of a judge; but those things didn't happen; and soon enough, Duncan grew big and strong, too big and strong to whip. One famous night, when Buster stripped off his belt and ordered Duncan to assume the position, the boy turned and knocked him cold. After that, Buster prudently adjusted his approach. He wanted a victim, not a sparring partner. Now, he acted as though he was Duncan's best friend, his champion against a hostile world. The hostile world was still mostly Buster himself, of course, something Duncan must have known well, but you couldn't have proved that by the new, protective father Buster had become. If you believed him.

It's a thing we see in families more than you might think we would. We see parents who go to bed as devils and wake up as angels – guardian angels: defenders, friends. We see homes where life goes overnight from a Golden Gloves bout to the Teddy Bears' picnic. People are strange, ain't they?

In the office I got Buster sitting down in the visitor's chair. Then I made a little play of hunting for the coffee. I looked here and there. I opened the office door and shouted down the hall for Evelyn. Time for some de-escalation.

'We got coffee?' I asked Evelyn.

''Course we do,' she shouted back.

'Where is it, then?'

'Right there where you're at.'

'No, it ain't,' I said.

Evelyn sighed. 'Just a minute,' she called. 'I'll look.' She didn't move. She sat at her desk. Evelyn and I had run this routine a hundred times on a hundred irate taxpayers demanding action of one kind and another. I turned to Buster. 'Evvy'll find it,' I said. 'She probably did something with it.'

'I don't want any god damned coffee,' Buster said. 'I want to see my son. He's supposed to be at Clara's. He ain't. That god damned school he goes to let out. He ain't there.

Something's going on. Talked to my ex in California. She says you probably know what it is. So, again, where the fuck is my son?'

'He's at Holiday's in Mount Nebo with his girlfriend from school. Homer Patch is there with them, too.'

'What girlfriend?' Buster asked. 'I don't know about any girlfriend. You mean a *girlfriend* girlfriend?'

'I don't know, Buster,' I said. 'Ask Duncan.'

'Fucking-A well right I'll ask him,' said Buster. What is he – what are they – doing at Holiday's?'

I opened a drawer in the credenza. 'Here's the coffee!' I said. '*It's okay*,' I called to Evelyn, who had long since returned to her paperback.

'Milk and sugar?' I asked Buster.

'What?'

'In your coffee. You want milk? Sugar?'

'Two sugars god damn it,' said Buster.

I fixed Buster's coffee and set it down in front of him on the desk.

'How is that?' I asked him. 'Is that okay? Not too much sugar?'

'Yes, it's okay,' said Buster, without having tasted the coffee.

'Good, good,' I said.

I poured a cup for myself and took it around the desk. I sat. Then I told Buster the whole story. I saw no reason not to. I told him about Duncan and Pamela's running away from her stepfather. I told him about Armentrout and his little team sent to find the couple, or at least the girl, about their wrecking Duncan and Pamela's campsite in Constance Truax's woods, their wrecking the cabin at the Hideaway. I described the fireworks at Cola's. I mentioned

Pamela's mother, who would soon be taking her out of the whole situation. Buster sat unmoving and listened to all I had to say. He never touched his coffee.

'I blame that fancy-ass rich kid's school,' said Buster when I had finished. 'All he got there's a big head. Thinks he's King Shit. Thinks he's too good for his own.'

He might be right about that, I thought, but what I said was, 'I know it, Buster. I know it: it's hard when your kids change.' I hoped Buster wouldn't ask me how the hell I thought I knew that, not having any kids, but all he said was, 'God damn right, it is.'

I went on. 'A fellow tries to raise his boy up straight,' I said, 'give him what he needs, and then, he changes. Just changes. It's like he's kidnapped. Ain't it?' I asked Buster.

'Fucking kidnapped,' said Buster, and proceeded to jump from the teachers and masters and so on at St. Bartholomew's to Armentrout and his heavy lifters.

'One thing,' said Buster. 'The girl? I don't give a shit about the girl. It's Dunc. If any of those bastards thinks he's going to hassle my boy – well, he's wrong, that's all. I will do what I have to do to protect my son. You say some city guy has a squad up here after Dunc? I say, bring them. Bring them the fuck on.'

Big talk ran in the March family, it seemed, big and dirty. Good to see old traditions getting passed on, ain't it?

'Leave it, Buster,' I said. 'Let us look out for Duncan. That's our job, not yours.'

'Been doing great with it, too, haven't you?' Buster said. 'Look, Sheriff, here's what it is: I'm going up to Holiday's, hear all this from Dunc, see he's okay. He'd fucking better be, too. If he is, then maybe I'll stay up there and help out. Maybe I won't. Maybe I'll bring Dunc home. Maybe

I'll go looking for them who's looking for Dunc. I can go where I want. It's a free country, ain't it?'

'Free as a fucking butterfly,' I said.

Well, as a de-escalation, if the job on Rhumba back there scored a 9, this today was 2, at best. Buster might have been a little calmer for our talk, but not much. He was ready to take on Armentrout's heavy lifters, and the Red Army with them. He was ready to take on Armentrout, himself, even Armentrout's boss, Rex Lord. Buster worried me. He didn't care about Armentrout's power, about Lord's money. He'd go straight through them – or anyway he'd try. That means nothing but trouble. Wingate used to say it: a poor man kicks another poor man, and nobody knows; a rich man kicks a poor man, and nobody cares. A poor man kicks a rich man, and there's hell to pay.

Worst of all, Buster hadn't drunk any coffee. If you have an indoor setting, an office, say, where coffee is available, and your subject don't drink your coffee, that's no de-escalation.

***

Buster wasn't going to be the only pissed-off parent on my plate that morning, it looked like. When he'd stomped out of my office, Evelyn buzzed me to say Addison and Carlotta were out front wanting to see me. I had them in, got us a round of coffee. At least they took coffee. While I was seeing to the coffee, I snuck a look at Addison so Carlotta couldn't see. Addison was stone: not a smile, not a glance, not a raised eyebrow. Uh-oh.

I took my seat behind my desk. 'Thanks for stopping by,' I said. Affable on wheels. 'What can I do for you folks this morning?' I asked Addison and Carlotta.

'Your job,' said Carlotta.

'Say again?'

'You can do your job, Sheriff,' said Carlotta. 'I've been up here for two days. I've talked to Pamela. I've talked to her thoroughly unsuitable young man. I even got Addison to show me that awful motel. That place belongs in Iraq.'

'I wouldn't know,' I said.

'What were you thinking of, putting Pamela somewhere like that?' Carlotta demanded.

'Thinking of keeping her and Duncan March safe while we see about the people who are after them.'

'*See about* them? You've done exactly nothing. And your way of keeping them safe, after putting them in that hellhole, is to get them into the middle of some appalling gunfight, and then, now, to lock them up off in the woods. Is that about right, Sheriff?'

'They ain't locked up,' I said.

'Let Lucian do his job, Lottie,' said Addison.

'Do his job? Why else am I here if not to see him do his job? He won't. He can't.'

She turned to me. 'You haven't the manpower,' she said. 'You think you can run this business by yourself. You can't. You need help.'

'Call the Staties,' said Addison.

'Staties?' Carlotta asked him.

'Vermont State Police,' said Addison. 'Call them, Lucian – or she will,' with a nod toward Carlotta.

Carlotta and Addison took themselves off. I sat for a minute and looked out the window. I couldn't fault Carlotta. As she said, reinforcements were needed. Still, it didn't set right with me. I hated it. I hated having to have Capt. Farrabaugh and his uniforms carrying my water for me. Farrabaugh and his chain of command, his fancy lingo, his bosses in high places. I recalled that Nachtigal business a couple of years back. Farrabaugh and his Boy Scouts had read me out of an operation in my jurisdiction, my bailiwick, my home: no reason, no excuse, no apology – just out.

Now, I guessed, Carlotta and Addison were right. I needed to call Farrabaugh. But I didn't have to do it gladly. And I didn't have to do it yet. I have told about Wingate, how stubborn he is. Well, he ain't the only one, is he?

16
Three Weeks in Philadelphia

'But, darling,' said Carlotta. 'Don't you see? It is. It's exactly like that. That joke.'

'What joke?' Addison asked her.

'That Philadelphia joke,' said Carlotta. She was being Lady Bountiful that evening, treating Addison, Clemmie and me to dinner at the inn. Carlotta had been in town for three days, and she was showing symptoms of withdrawal from fancy, overpriced food served on heavy white tablecloths. The inn wasn't up to her accustomed metropolitan standard, of course, but it was the valley's best shot, and, 'What can they do to *côtelettes d'agneau à l'anglaise*?' asked Carlotta.

'What's that?' I asked.

'Lamb chops,' said Clemmie.

'Philadelphia joke?' Addison asked. 'Oh, yes, of course. W. C. Fields.'

I caught Clemmie's eye and nodded toward the entrance of the dining room. Carl Armentrout had just come in and was being shown to a corner table for one across the room. His usual table, Clemmie said, Armentrout by now having been a less than well-liked but profitable guest of the inn for some days. He sat and looked around the room, saw us, rose, and came over to our table.

'Lottie!' said Armentrout. 'You're here? Well, of course you are. How are the Alps?' He nodded to Clemmie, Addison and me, but he kept his attention on Carlotta.

'The Alps are there, Carl,' said Carlotta. If Armentrout were water, she would have froze him.

'It's been too long,' said Armentrout. 'You look wonderful. You're here for Pammy? She'll turn up, I'm sure.'

'I'm sure she will,' said Carlotta.

'Already has, maybe?' Armentrout looked narrowly at Carlotta.

'You haven't seen her, I don't suppose? Rex is very concerned.'

'Poor Rex,' said Carlotta.

'You've talked to Rex? You have, haven't you?' Armentrout asked her.

'Run along, Carl,' said Carlotta.

'Darling, what a reptile,' said Carlotta after Armentrout had left us to return to his table. 'What an insect. I never trusted him, never. Rex always said I was being foolish. We'll see who was foolish. What a snake.

'Still, you have to feel sorry for him, a bit, don't you?' she went on. 'Stuck up here day after day, waiting for word from his, uh, staff? I mean, he's not a total idiot. How bored he must be.'

'There you go again,' Addison said. 'Who's bored, besides you? You don't get it. You talk as though it's a desert up here. But we're here.' He nodded at Clemmie and me. 'We're here. In the valley. We're not idiots, either. And we're not bored.'

'Sometimes, just a little, maybe,' said Clemmie.
'Oh, don't misunderstand me,' Carlotta said. 'I know why you love it here. I see its beauty, its peace. The people. Everybody is very nice. But, darling, be honest. Really, when you've said that, you've said it all. There's nothing else. It's as I said: the Philadelphia joke.'
'What's the Philadelphia joke?' Clemmie asked.
'It's an old W. C. Fields routine,' said Addison. 'Fields announces a contest, or a raffle. First prize is a week in Philadelphia. Second prize is two weeks in Philadelphia. Third prize, three weeks in Philadelphia.'
'But, yes, darling, that's it, exactly,' said Carlotta. 'There's what you see and do every day, all very well, but then there's nothing further. You wait for the next step, the next thing. There isn't one. There's no movement. There's no plot. It's like a wax museum. There you are. There you have it. That's your valley: three weeks in Philadelphia.'
'I don't get it,' I said.

***

Wingate surprised me. 'Clemmie thinks Armentrout's behind this whole thing,' I told him. 'Thinks Lord's not really part of it at all.'
'Lord's the rich fellow in New York?' Wingate asked me.
'That's right. Rex Lord. The runaway girl's stepfather.'
'And the other's his lawyer?'
'That's right.'
'Could be she's got something, your Clementine,' said Wingate.
'She does?' I asked him. 'How do you figure?'

'Well,' said Wingate. 'Ask yourself: who makes out, here? If Mr. Lord wins, he gets the girl back, right? Fine, but that puts him where he started. There's no gain. If Mr. – What was the name?'

'Armentrout,' I said.

'If Mr. Armentrout wins, he gets a big payday. He collects. That's what's called incentive, ain't it?'

'I don't see it,' I said. 'Lord's Armentrout's meal ticket. It's a big ticket, a big meal. He's Armentrout's boss.'

'So what if he's his boss,' asked Wingate. 'Lots of people don't like their boss. They pretend to, but they don't, really. You don't know that, see, because you had a good boss. Me. I was your boss.'

'You were?' I said. 'I couldn't always tell.'

'I know you couldn't,' said Wingate. 'Like you can't tell now which one you're up against: Lord or Armentrout. Be good to know that, wouldn't it?'

'It would,' I said.

'How are you going to find out?'

'I was getting ready to ask you that,' I said.

'Was me?' said Wingate. 'I'd go to your father-in-law. Lawyer Jessup.'

'Addison?' I said. 'Where's he fit? He's got nothing to do with Armentrout. I guess he said he knew Lord years back, but I didn't get the idea Addison knew him well then – or knows him at all now.'

'You didn't get the idea don't mean there's no idea to get,' said Wingate. 'Does it?'

'No.'

'Besides,' Wingate went on, 'Lawyer Jessup's an educated man. A professional man. He's not just a dumb, ignorant woodchuck like you and me. Be good to get his view, is all.'

'It would,' I said.

***

'You're sure?' Addison asked. He held the bottle of White Horse out in my direction. We were on the screened back porch at Addison's. Addison tilted the bottle toward me and raised his eyebrows. I shook my head.

'On duty,' I said. Addison sighed and fixed himself a drink.

'What I don't get?' I said. 'If Clemmie's right and Armentrout's plan is to find the girl, Pammy, and hold her until Lord pays up for her, how's that supposed to work? She's not Lord's daughter. He don't seem like the generous type. She's practically accused him of I don't know what godawful carrying on. Why would he bail her out?'

'I can help you there,' said Addison. 'He'll bail her out because of Carlotta. Lottie will tell him he'd damned well better come across – or else.'

'Or else, what?'

'Or else she'll make certain interested parties – in the government, in the courts, in the press – aware of certain information she has concerning certain dealings Rex Lord has had over the years, certain private projects that Rex would far rather remain private. You see what I'm saying?'

'I see.'

'The thing is,' Addison went on, 'Carlotta started out working for Rex Lord. This is when I first knew her, in New York, after she'd chucked Roger DeMorgan. She was

Lord's Personal Assistant. Do you know what a Personal Assistant is?'

'I know I don't have one,' I said. 'Don't need one, probably.'

'Wrong,' said Addison. 'Everybody needs one. Your Personal Assistant's your brain, your memory, your dresser, your scheduler, your accountant, your secretary, your procurer...'

'What's a procurer?' I asked Addison.

'Never mind,' said Addison. 'You don't have one of them, either. At least, I hope you don't. At least not now. Point is, Carlotta, as Lord's PA and later as his wife, was in a position to see all the way down to the bottom of the well. She knows all the secrets – or, at least, she knows more than enough of them. If she tells Lord to unbelt – for Pamela, for the Humane Society, for anybody – then he'll unbelt. Depend on it. Lottie's got Lord by the short ones. And he knows it.'

'You wouldn't think it of her,' I said.

'Don't underestimate Lottie,' said Addison. 'She may swan around as though she was the Duchess of Dingleberry and hadn't a brain in her head. Don't believe it. Lottie's plenty smart, and plenty tough.'

'Sounds like you knew her pretty well,' I said.

'I ought to have,' said Addison. 'Lottie and I were engaged to be married.'

'You were? What happened?'

'What happened was I invited her up here. See my home. Meet my people. Seemed like a good idea at the time. Wasn't. Was a big mistake. Carlotta took a look around, took another, asked me, in a very quiet, low, deliberate voice if I intended for us to live here after we were married.

I said I did. Long pause. The next day, she was on her way back to New York. The next year, she married Rex Lord.'

'And you married Clemmie's mom.'

'Monica,' said Addison. 'That was later. She didn't much like it up here, either. Funny about that.'

'Maybe it wasn't the valley they didn't like,' I said.

'What else?'

'Maybe it was you.'

'Not possible,' said Addison. 'As for Lottie and Rex Lord: he had what she wanted. She went after it, and she got it. Well played, Lottie.'

Addison grew silent. He sat gazing deep into his glass of White Horse.

'What?' I asked him.

'Carlotta,' said Addison. 'I still think about her, you know? We were good together. We got on. In every way, if you take my meaning. Except for one way: the setting. The woods, the hills, the little villages, the winter. Carlotta wasn't up for them. She was funny about it, really. She said she felt, up here, as though she was on a stage set. Everything was made of painted canvas and paper, as though she could walk up to somebody's cow standing in a field and punch her hand right through it. She could try to go through a door and bump into the wall: no door there, only a picture of a door.'

'Some cows I've known,' I said, 'if she tried to punch a hole in them, she'd find out in a hurry whether they were real.'

'Good old Lottie,' said Addison. 'Clearly, it wouldn't have worked.

'Still...'

***

Carlotta soon got her wish about rolling up the heavy guns in the form of the Staties. The day after her call at my office, Dwight Farrabaugh paid us a surprise visit, and it wasn't my birthday.

'We need to talk, Lucian,' Captain Farrabaugh said. He took the visitor's chair in my office.

'What about?'

'About the way your little patch of ground draws in such a weird mix of foreign bad guys. Can you tell me why that might be? You're practically the perps' UN, down here. Why is that?'

'I don't know, Captain,' I said. 'Good luck? Fall foliage?'

'Couple of years back,' Dwight went on, 'it was those crazy Russians or whatever they were. Now, this.'

'Now, what?' I asked. Dwight put a manila envelope on the desk between us and shoved it across to me. He nodded at it. 'Now, these two,' he said.

I picked up the envelope and took out two photos, apparently taken from a standard police identification document, but reduced to front and profile views of two men, with their heights shown on the scale, in feet and inches, at the side of the shot. One was a big fellow, six-five, with a hooked beak of a nose and a rough face, deeply pock-marked. The other was Armentrout's driver: small, five-eight, with plump, smooth cheeks and little bright eyes. That was all Dwight had given me: no names, no records, no dates, no sign of where the sheets had originated.

'The large gent is a Cuban,' Dwight told me. 'His name is Hector Mendes Colon. He's fifty, operates mainly in New York and Mexico City. He's a bill collector. Call it that. A bill collector, and a kind of general-purpose handyman in the strongarm line. And then more yet. According to my information, Mendes has at least two murder warrants in Mexico – but down there, who doesn't, you know? Anyway, a useful man. Set his hand to anything, Hector will.

'His friend is called Bray. Louis Bray. At least, we think that's his name. It's one of his names, anyway. Brit. Londoner. We think: don't know for sure. His age? Don't know. His line? Same as the *senor*. You wouldn't think it, would you? Pudgy little fellow like that? Don't be fooled. According to my information, if Bray thinks it's worth his while, and if he gets revved up, he makes Mendes look like a Chihuahua puppy.'

'You keep saying *According to your information*,' I said. 'What is your information? Where from?'

'Come on, Lucian,' said Dwight. 'You know I can't get into any of that with you.'

'Oh, right,' I said. 'I forgot. This is more of your famous *teamwork*, ain't it? Come on, yourself.'

Dwight shrugged. He looked out the window, not at me.

'Give it up, Captain,' I said. 'You'll feel better, you know you will.'

Dwight looked at me. Then he stood and went to close the office door. He returned to his chair, which he hitched closer to the desk between us.

'Got a phone call earlier,' said Dwight. 'From higher up.'

'Your commander?'

'No,' said Dwight. 'Higher.'

'Higher?'

'Higher.'

'Attorney General's office?'

Dwight pointed at the ceiling.

'What are you saying?' I asked Dwight. 'The Governor?'

'Keep going.'

'Really?' I asked.

Dwight nodded. 'The caller – don't ask – advised that Mendes and Bray are known to be in your area of operations. They've been observed and confirmed. It's Mendes and Bray, all right, but what they're about we don't know. Do you?'

'Little vacation in the country?'

Dwight didn't dignify that. 'Sheriff?' he said.

'Okay,' I said. 'I probably know what you're asking. I know the little one, Bray. At least I've seen him.'

'Where?' Dwight asked.

'Before we get to that, let me ask you a couple. Do you know a guy named Rex Lord?'

'Negative,' said Dwight. 'Oh, unless you mean the billionaire. That one?'

'That one,' I said.

'Then, still negative, except for seeing him in the papers.'

'Do you know a lawyer named Armentrout? Carl Armentrout?'

'Negative,' said Dwight.

'Or by another name? Bascom? Bassett?'

'Negative,' said Dwight. 'Your turn.'

So I told Dwight my sad tale of woe: the runaways, the people looking for them, including Armentrout, our efforts to keep the kids secure – through to now and the arrival of Duncan's old man, Buster, all ready to come charging in on his eighteen-wheeler and bring the whole business crashing down around us.

'I don't like that last guy at all,' said Dwight when I'd done.

'I'm not crazy about him, myself.'

'Listen, Lucian,' said Dwight, 'for him, for you, for all your people: stay away from these two. Stay right away. You get that? You have a line on them, you call us. That's it. That's all you do. For the rest, you stand down. Mendes and Bray are strictly, strictly on a Do Not Approach basis for you.'

That was Dwight: all business. Partly it was a matter of – call it corps identity. The State Police and our local sheriff's departments are on the same side, but we're raised and educated differently, like the Army and the Marines, like dogs and cats. The Staties have the budgets, they have the scientific and technical horses, they have the manpower, the equipment, the rolling stock. They have the prestige. We have the fun. Dwight sees that, and sometimes it makes him bear down harder than he needs to. He didn't have to tell me not to approach Mendes and Bray. I had no intention of approaching them.

But even so, I probably knew the end: I didn't have to approach them. They approached me.

17
A Heap of Cinders

In the end, they caught me in the oldest trap of them all: the Lady in Distress. That Friday afternoon, going into Memorial Day weekend, I was on my way home when Evelyn came on the radio. She should have knocked off same time I did.

'What are you doing there?' I asked her. 'Go home.'

'Susie's car conked out. She's running late. I told her I'd fill in. I'll leave when she's sorted out.'

'What's the call?' I asked Evelyn.

'Stranded motorist. River Road. By Houston's,' said Evelyn. 'Easy one.'

'Okay,' I said. 'I've got it.' Now I ask myself, do I recall thinking Evelyn sounded a little off, a little strange? Maybe. But I didn't know. And, I reckoned, if you've just watched your Friday evening go up the flue, you might be sounding a little off, yourself.

Couple of miles out the River Road, here was a nice new Lexus pulled onto the shoulder. New York plates. Tinted windows so you couldn't see inside. Hood raised and propped open. Young woman standing helplessly beside the car, waving shyly at me. I drove in behind her. Good-looking girl, redhead, slim, thirty-five, wearing the kind of Western cowboy-style jeans that cost more than most cowboys make in a year.

I got down from the truck and went along the side of the Lexus to the young woman. 'Out of gas?' I asked her. She didn't answer, but only gave me an odd little smile. Then the rear driver's-side door opened just behind me, and the passenger got out. I hadn't been able to see him because of the darkened windows. Uh-oh. It was Mendes, the Cuban, a.k.a. Hector, the larger of the two gorillas with Armentrout. Dwight Farrabaugh's mugshot was a good likeness. Hector was heavy and hard, and his pitted face looked misshapen, somehow, as though he'd been in a fire or a bad crash.

'Sheriff? Are you armed?' Mendes asked me. A little bit of an accent. Spanish? Why not? He was cool and calm, master of the situation, of all situations.

I shook my head. Mendez nodded toward the young woman, who came from the front of the Lexus to us.

'Position your hands on top of the car, and step back, Sheriff,' said Mendes. 'You know what to do.'

I knew what to do. I grasped the roof of the car and leaned onto it on my arms. The girl came up behind me and proceeded to give me a very thorough, professional pat-down. She not only patted, she poked and squeezed. She went up and down, high and low, around and between, both hands. Not even Clemmie did that kind of a job, or not unless she was in a real good mood and had a couple of glasses of wine in her. In a minute the young woman stepped back and gave Hector a little nod.

Hector brought my arms down and held them. The girl took a pair of handcuffs from her jeans pocket and cuffed my wrists together behind my back. She looked at Hector. Hector nodded, and the girl closed the hood of the Lexus, got in behind the wheel, started the engine, and drove off down River Road. I never heard her speak a word. I never saw her again.

Hector took one of my arms and guided me to my truck. He helped me get up into the passenger's seat. Then he took the driver's seat and got us rolling, doing a U-turn to get headed away from Cardiff and the highway and toward the hills, toward Mount Nebo and Holiday's. Not good.

I was hurting. Hector's helper had cuffed me high and tight behind, so my shoulders felt like they were getting ready to pop out of their sockets. I leaned forward in the seat, trying to relieve them. Hector didn't like that.

'Sit back, Sheriff,' he said. 'Enjoy the ride.'

'Can't you ease off these cuffs a hair, or let me sit different?' I asked. 'This is wicked uncomfortable, you know it?'

'Your comfort is not of concern to me, Sheriff,' said Hector.

'I got that,' I said. We drove on, clear across the valley. By the time we reached the turnoff for Holiday's, it was getting dark.

Hector parked my truck along the road around the bend from the sugarhouse. He got me out. As he did, he gave my handcuffs a sharp jerk upward that nearly made me sing out. 'Sheriff?' he said. 'Do I have your attention? You go first. Do not run. Do not fight. Do not think of it. You see?' He drew back his shirttail to show me a little automatic pistol in a waistband holster. 'You would not get far,' he said. 'You see that?'

'I see that,' I said.

We left the road and set out into the woods. Evidently, Hector wanted to come around and approach the sugarhouse from the rear. He stayed close, two paces behind me. Yes, he had me covered pretty good.

I didn't have much of a play on any line, unless his gun was for show. I didn't think it was. So we bushwhacked on.

'Do you work for Armentrout?' I asked Hector after we had gone maybe a quarter-mile.

'I work for no one, Sheriff,' said Hector.

'Self-employed, then?' I said. 'Good for you. Good to be your own boss, I'll bet. I wouldn't know. I work for the county, always have. But I'm with you. For sure, I wouldn't work for Armentrout for any money, I know that. I don't care: I don't like the man. It's a question of pride, ain't it? There's more important things than a paycheck, you know?'

'Sheriff?' Hector said.

'What?'

'*Callate!*' said Hector. 'Shut up, Sheriff.'

Okay. No de-escalating this one, it didn't look like.

In another fifteen minutes, I stopped and pointed ahead and to our left. A light burned off in the woods. Somebody had brought a lantern. By now it was nearly full dark. You could barely see the shape of the sugarhouse with its lighted window, just ahead.

'That's it,' I told Hector. 'That's Holiday's sugarhouse.'

Hector looked. 'All right,' he said. 'Quietly, Sheriff.'

We approached the sugarhouse. I could see through the window Duncan and Pamela standing by the far wall. Nobody else, yet.

Hector put a hand on my shoulder. I stopped. He drew his little pistol and held it in his right hand. His left hand he put lightly on my back, fingers spread, and urged me forward. Together that way, with a target on my chest the size of Pennsylvania, or so it felt like to me, and another on my back the size of Ohio, we advanced on Holiday's sugarhouse, reached the little deck or porch in front, crossed it, and opened the door.

We walked into – silence. The sugarhouse was a single room, twenty feet square, darkly lit by a couple of railroad lanterns, and quiet as a Quaker meeting. I took a quick look around. Five people. Duncan and Pamela stood against the end wall of the building. Duncan's hands were cuffed behind. Pamela was free, but she didn't move. She held the case for her flute in both arms against her chest. Homer and Buster March were seated on the floor, back to back, shackled together behind by their wrists, as I was, and tied around their shoulders by a length of rope, for good measure. Seated and bound, the two of them looked like a single creature, ancient and monstrous: a giant spider or crab. Buster was bleeding from a cut on his scalp. He must have tried to crash the party and been put down hard, evidently by Carl Armentrout's chauffeur, the Britisher Capt. Farrabaugh's information called Louis Bray.

Bray himself was in the middle of the room, sitting perched on the old brick fire arch. In his black suit and tie and white shirt, he looked like the junior partner in a firm of undertakers. He held a shotgun across his knees. He wasn't happy.

'You're late,' Bray said to Hector.

'Plenty of time,' said Hector.

Homer looked up at me from his place on the floor. 'They followed Buster,' he said. 'I ought to have been ready for them. I wasn't.'

'You couldn't have been,' I said.

'*Callate*!' said Hector.

'Where's Carl?' the little chauffeur asked Hector.

'Hah,' said Hector. 'Senor Carl is safe, you can be sure. Did you expect him to do any of the real work? We'll pick him up on our way out. Now, then.' He turned to me. 'Sheriff,' he said, 'our business is at an end. We leave you four here. Needless to say, you will report to your superiors about my colleague and me. Needless to say, it will make no difference to anything. We will be long gone. I, for one, won't be sorry.'

'I will,' I said. 'I'm going to miss the daylights out of you.'

'Senor Louis will now manacle you to the wall,' said Hector. Bray put his shotgun aside, let himself down from his spot on the fire arch, and drew a pair of handcuffs from his pocket. Those fellows must have had stock in the handcuff company, or I hope they did.

'What about the girl?' I asked Hector.

'She goes with us,' said Hector.

'*No*,' said Pamela.

'No,' said Duncan.

'No,' said Buster.

'*Who's that*?' asked Homer, and he looked toward the door.

'Who's that?' asked Bray, pivoting in the same direction.

'Who's that?' I asked, and turned toward the door, myself – in time to see that whole side of the room, with everything before, behind, around and above me, blow up.

There came a quick banging rush of steps on the porch outside, and then one whole wall of the room shuddered as in an earthquake, bulged inward, bulged further, gave out, and, with an explosive cracking and ripping, burst into a storm of broken timbers, siding, wall studs and window glass.

I saw a large, low form crash at top speed through the shattered wall and into the room. For a second, I thought it was some kind of vehicle, a pallet skid, or a golf cart. Then I saw: it was Big John, the monster forest hog, at large again. I sprang for the safety of the fire arch, as Big John went about dismantling the room, the walls, the windows, the whole sugarhouse.

He blew through the building like a tornado. He body-checked Hector violently into the side wall. Hector hit hard and sank to the floor unconscious. The little fellow, Bray, tried to make a run for it, but John caught him with a tusk and hurled him the length of the room. Bray landed like a child's rag doll and lay where he fell, out of the fight.

Pamela opened her flute case and came out fast with Cola's Army .45, evidently hoping to get in on the action. Unfortunately, the pistol went off before she was set. (So much for Cola's firearms instruction.) The wild shot hit one of the lanterns, which exploded, spreading burning kerosene over one end of the room. Homer, Buster and the two young people had taken shelter with me on, under and around the fire arch. We watched Big John race around the circuit of the room like a crazed greyhound at the dog track, then dash through the growing fire and barrel into the building's far wall, which burst as the first wall had and let the maddened boar, leading a trail of sparks and burning debris, break through it and go tearing off into the darkness.

Built of old dry pine lumber as it was, the sugarhouse burned like a match. Time to go. 'Keys,' I called to Pamela. She ran to the prostrate, senseless Hector and went into his pockets. When she had the handcuff keys, she unlocked me, and I unlocked Homer, Buster and

Duncan. Then the five of us dragged Hector and Bray out of the sugarhouse by the heels, no more than a couple of yards ahead of the fire. We got clear of the building and stood around in front, watching the sugarhouse go up in flames.

'I always said we'd ought to burned it, years back,' I reminded Homer.

'What, and miss all this?' Homer asked.

He and I shackled Hector and Bray to a couple of trees for safekeeping. Homer was for taking them out right then and turning them over to the State Police, but I thought we'd better wait here. We didn't know how badly hurt Hector and Bray were. And, plus, I reasoned, somebody would see the fire and call it in, so we'd have reinforcements soon enough. We decided to sit tight.

We didn't sit for long. Vehicles coming around the bend, coming fast. Red lights, blue lights. The roof of the sugarhouse had fallen in. Now about all that was left of the structure was the brick fire arch and an acrid heap of charred and blackened timbers, poorly lit by what flames broke out here and there, then died down.

Deputy Treat came up to me; following him, three Staties, two medics from the Valley Rescue, and the chief of the Mount Nebo Volunteer Fire Department. Treat looked over the sugarhouse, looked at Hector and Bray. They had come to. The medics were examining them.

'What happened, Sheriff?' Deputy Treat asked me.

'These two were after Pamela,' I told him. 'They had us locked down. They were ready to take her when that Christly pig came in like a runaway train and blew everything to flinders.'

'Big John?' asked Treat. 'No shit?'

'No shit,' I said.

'I've been looking for him all day,' said Treat. 'He was in Dead River this morning.'

'That's a fast-moving hog,' I said. 'That's a hog that gets around the infield.' I was starting to feel easier.

What about the fire?' the Mount Nebo chief asked me.

'These two fellows had a lantern. It got shot out, broke, set the place afire.'

'I'm sure glad I got here in time,' said the chief, looking over the smoking hill of hot coals that had been the sugarhouse. 'It looks like we saved another heap of cinders, don't it?'

'Good work,' I told him.

So we turned Hector and Bray over to the Staties for delivery to Captain Farrabaugh at the barracks, and made ready to close the operation down. Bray had a gash on his thigh where Big John had tusked him, and Hector had a bump on his head, but they were healthy enough. Hector, in fact, was feeling pretty trig.

'Why do you waste your people's time, Sheriff?' he asked me.

'You know we will be back on our way in a couple of hours. You know you can't charge us. We have done nothing to be charged with.'

'You're too modest,' I said. 'Let's see: you've abducted a public officer and held him at gunpoint. That would be me – and the constable here, too, come to that,' I nodded to Homer. 'Then, you've conspired to kidnap this young woman. You've caused malicious damage to property, including arson, you've engaged in threatening conduct. And all that's just local. Where you're going now, they reckon you're wanted on I don't know how many charges, in how many places. They're going to be glad to see you, all right. They're not going to want to cut you loose for some time.'

Now, as a matter of fact, none of that sounded too strong, even to me. Truth was, I reckoned Hector was about right: Armentrout would spring him and Bray pretty quick. But I'd bet they were all done up here, in any case. Their plan to hold Pamela for ransom from her father wouldn't fly far once Rex Lord found out about Armentrout's double game. Hector and Bray wouldn't go to jail, or not for long, but neither would they be back in the valley. I'd settle for that. Sure, I would. In my line of work, you can't usually make a bad thing good, or even much better than it was; but sometimes you can make a bad thing go be bad someplace else for a while. If you can get that, I say, take it.

So we went down the mountain in the dark. At the turnout we broke up and went our separate ways. The troopers took charge of the two prisoners. Deputy Treat offered to stop at our department and start in writing up our report of the whole business. I didn't stop him. I was shot. It had been a long day. I set out for home, a cold beer, and Clemmie. But, even now, I didn't quite make it. One last card remained to be turned.

Treat came on the radio. He was at the sheriff's office. There he'd found, not Evelyn filling in for Susie, her night-time partner, whose car had broken down, but Susie herself, locked in the supply closet, banging on the door, hungry, thirsty, her back teeth afloat and mad as hell.

There was nothing wrong with Susie's car, as Evelyn had told me there was. Susie had got to work as usual. When she came on duty, Evelyn had asked her to get some forms out of the closet. Susie had gone in there, Evelyn had slammed the door on her, locked it and taken off. She wasn't home. She wasn't anywhere – except possibly on her way to some distant beach, where she'd soon be enjoying a fancy drink with the Lady in Distress who had kicked this whole day off. She was gone, too.

18
Kittens in the Oven

Things were breaking up. On the weekend, Deputy Treat had driven Pamela over to the Maine Coast to stay with a friend from school for the balance of the summer. Carlotta offered to pay him, but the deputy wouldn't hear of it.

'He doesn't want pay,' said Clemmie. 'He wants to be with Pamela.'

'Still cranking the handle on that rig, are you?' I asked Clemmie. 'Give it up. That car won't start. The deputy ain't interested. He ain't in the game. I told you and told you.'

'We'll see,' said Clemmie. 'I'm counting your hundred dollars right now.'

'Don't spend it yet, Miz Jessup,' I said.

'I think I will,' said Clemmie. 'I think I'll put it to a down payment on the new deck. Think I'll call Rory tomorrow.'

Clemmie was at the kitchen sink washing the china. She picked up the sugar bowl and commenced drying it on a towel. I was in the doorway. I was talking to her back.

'The hell you will,' I said.

Clemmie turned to face me. She held the sugar bowl with the dishtowel in both hands.

'Like I said before,' I went on. 'I ain't going to pay your ninth-grade sweetie and the half-naked bodybuilders he hires for help to come up here and put on a beef parade for my wife.'

'What bodybuilders?' Clemmie demanded. 'You're crazy. They're college kids. Not even that: high school.'

'Younger the better for you, right?'

'Be careful, Lucian,' Clemmie said.

'You be careful.'

'Me? I thought we were talking about Rory's crew.'

'We're talking about a lot of things,' I said. 'We're talking about Rory's crew. We're talking about Rory, himself, too, ain't we? I'm sure you'd love to have Rory climbing all over the house, banging nails. Just banging away.'

'Have you gone completely nuts?' Clemmie asked me. 'Rory and I? We were ten.'

'Well, there's where you went wrong, ain't it?' I said. 'You missed out. You ought to have jumped on him when you had the chance. I understand old Rory does very well for himself. You should have sewn him up. By now, we'd all be rich.'

'Shut up,' said Clemmie.

'Or, I'll tell you,' I went on. 'How about Loren? Loren Hinckley. The Dartmouth man. Remember him? Sure, you do. What's old Loren doing now? Hey, maybe he's a builder, too. You like builders, right? Rory, Loren: we could get them both up here. Have a party. How about that?'

Clemmie took a step toward me. I saw I might have pulled the pin all the way out this time. Clemmie dropped the dishtowel to the floor. Uh-oh. 'Hold it,' I said. 'Hold it, now.'

Too late. Clemmie drew back her arm with the sugar bowl held high, took aim, wound up, and let fly.

***

I unlocked the office safe, took out Cola's forty-five, laid it on the desk, and shoved it toward him, where he sat in the visitor's chair. Cola picked up the pistol, dropped the magazine, checked the chamber. 'Where's the shells?' he asked me.

'They're in a safe place,' I said. 'Which means not with you.'

'They're my property.'

'God damn you, Cola,' I said. 'I ought to stick that thing right up your ass. You know that?'

'You and which army, Sheriff?' asked Cola. He was well pleased with himself.

'What in the world were you thinking, giving that little girl a gun?'

'Thinking she needed to be able to defend herself, Sheriff,' said Cola. 'Like every other free-born citizen.'

'You could have gotten somebody killed,' I said. 'You didn't think of that?'

Cola shrugged.

'I suppose you're one of these damn fools thinks we'd all be so much safer if everybody carried a gun, ain't you?'

'Not everybody, Sheriff,' said Cola. 'Just me.'

'Get to hell out of my office,' I said. 'Go on, beat it.'

Cola took his time getting to his feet. He stuck the forty-five in his belt and turned toward the office door. I stopped him.

'Wait a minute,' I said. Cola paused. 'I heard you and the humane lady ran across Big John yesterday,' I said. 'That so?'

'We did more than run across him,' said Cola. 'We got him. We caught the son of a bitch, Sheriff.'

'What happened?'

'Some kids out squirrel hunting spotted John coming out of one of the caves other side of Round Mountain. They told Millie Pickens, and she got me. We went up there and waited at the mouth of the cave. I fired a couple of rounds. John came roaring out of there like a fucking volcano. Just boiling out of there. Well, Millie hit him with half a dozen supersize knockout darts, and down he went.'

'Where is he now?' I asked Cola. 'Back at Herbie's?'

'Herbie don't want him,' said Cola. 'Wouldn't take him back. Said he's all done with John and his escapes. I offered to make a peaceful and painless end to John right then and there, you know? Like I wanted to do back of my place with you, that time? But Millie said if I did, she'd do the same to me – minus the peaceful and painless. She's going to keep him. Make a pet of him.'

'A pet?'

'She says.'

'Some pet,' I said. Then, 'Since when are you and the humane lady so close? I wouldn't have said you hit it off, exactly, that other time.'

'We're working together now,' said Cola. 'You ought to have seen her when John came charging out of his hole, there. He came right at her. Millie just stood there pumping the darts into him: *phut, phut, phut*. John finally went down right at her feet. She never moved. Stand her ground? I guess she did. Balls on that gal? I was impressed.'

***

I know I ought not to have hit Clemmie with Rory O'Hara during our recent go-round. I certainly ought not to have hit her with Loren Hinkley. But when you're in a bar fight, you pick up the nearest bottle, and Rory, then, was near to me. He was on my mind.

He wasn't the only thing on my mind, either. There were others.

Carl Armentrout, for one. Needless to say, he was nowhere to be found. The night clerk at the inn said Armentrout had checked out in the grey first hours of the same morning his hired hands had come to grief at Holiday's. Armentrout had been picked up and driven off by a woman in a little car, a woman alone.

Well, it had to have been Evelyn, my loyal, competent despatcher. Can you believe it? All this time, no doubt well paid by Armentrout, Evelyn had been keeping him right up to the minute on our plans and movements with Duncan and Pamela. Evelyn had known everything, and she'd given it all to Armentrout. Now that their scheme had crashed, she came to smuggle Armentrout out of town ahead of us. I wouldn't have believed it if anything else had been possible. Evelyn had been working at the sheriff's department when I succeeded Wingate. We'd made such a good team, I'd thought. And here she sells out to a toad like Armentrout? How could she do that? To me? It don't do much for your faith.

At least there was one of us who was enjoying Evelyn's betrayal: Addison was tickled to death by the whole dirty business.

'Hell, Lucian,' he said, slapping me on the back as he made for the drinks table, 'you should be proud. I know I would be. You've hit the big time. You've got a mole. A regular woodchuck Kim Philby.'

'Who's Tim Philbrick?'

'Philby. The master spy. He's the one of your top people who you learn, too late, has secretly been working for the opposition all along. A traitor, a sleeper, a fifth column. Right here in the valley. Can you beat it?'

Addison was having a high old time. Why wouldn't he be? He don't have to run for office every couple of years on the basis that he knows his job, that he ain't a half-wit to be faked out by the switchboard girl.

***

Coming out of the hardware, I ran into Constance Truax. Tried to dodge – but no, she had me. 'May I have a minute, Sheriff,' she said.

Constance's old beater of a Chev pickup was parked at the kerb, so we went to it and leaned back against the tailgate to talk. It sometimes seems to me like two thirds of my job is done leaning on somebody's truck.

'I'm glad we met, Sheriff,' said Ms. Truax. 'I've been thinking about those people who were camping in my woods. The flute player? Do you remember them?'

'I remember,' I said.

'Who were they?' Ms. Truax asked me.

I paused. Asked straight out that way, the question wasn't easy to answer.

'Who were they?' I said. 'They were young people. Runaways, I guess you'd say. Boy and a girl, travelling together.'

'Local?'

'Not the girl. She was from away. The boy's Buster March's son. He's local. That's why they came here.'

'Buster March?' asked 'Ms. Truax. I had Buster March in school. I'm not surprised his son runs from him.'

'They weren't running from Buster, though,' I said.

'From whom, then?'

'People connected to the girl. People from the city.'

'Not good people, I'm guessing,' said Ms. Truax.

'No,' I said. 'Not good people.'

'Did they find her?'

'No.'

'So they're still here?'

'No,' I said. 'They went away.'

'That's good, then,' said Ms. Truax. 'You know, I've worried about those two. I've been afraid I'd gotten them in trouble by calling you in. I didn't, did I?'

'No,' I said. 'They were in trouble, but not from you.'

'And now they're safe?'

'It looks as though they would be, yes,' I told her.

'I miss the music,' said Ms. Truax. 'The flute. When they were up here, I came to like it. And now, do you know, I think I hear it still, some days. I think – I imagine – I hear that flute. But you say that can't be. You say it's gone.'

'Yes, ma'am,' I said. 'It's gone.'

I had to wonder at Constance Truax, hearing flute music way out in the woods where she was. It wasn't Pamela she was hearing. It wasn't anybody. Maybe Mrs. Truax spent too much time alone. Maybe she had popped a breaker. Or maybe she'd discovered you can get to places none of us guessed you could reach on cow parsnip.

***

Deputy Treat wants a day off. He's earned it, he'll get it, but of course we don't want to make it too easy for him, do we? We have to bounce him around a little first.

'Gee, Deputy,' I said. 'Didn't you just have a day off? Sure, you did. You went to Maine. And now you're back for another? This is a law enforcement organisation, here, you know? This ain't a sea cruise. It ain't a hotel, you check in and check out any time you like.'

'I know that, Sheriff,' said Treat. 'I wouldn't ask if it weren't important.'

'Well,' I said. 'I don't know. I guess it's okay. You'll have your pager, right? You'll be reachable?'

'I'm afraid I won't, Sheriff,' said Treat. 'I'm going to see Pammy.'

'Pammy?' I asked him. 'You just saw her, like I said. You drove her clear to Maine. Now you're going to see her again?'

'Come on, Sheriff,' said Treat. 'We're engaged. Or we will be when I get back.' He went into his pocket and took out a small box. He opened it and showed me a gold ring with a little green stone. 'See, there?' he asked me.

'You work fast, Deputy,' I said. 'What is she, sixteen?'

'Eighteen next month,' said Treat. 'We can wait.'

I stood up from the desk and held out my hand to Treat. 'Well, deputy,' I said, 'I guess it's congratulations and good luck, then, ain't it?'

'Thanks, Sheriff,' said the deputy. 'We both appreciate it.'

'It's a big step, marriage,' I said.

'It is,' said Treat.

'My advice?' I said. 'Keep loose. Keep loose, and don't forget to duck.'

'Is that about it, Sheriff?' Treat asked me. 'I should get going.'

'That's about it,' I said.

Treat turned to go. 'Well, I guess I'll be on my way, then,' he said.

'I'll see you in a couple of days, Sheriff.'

'I hope you got a good price on Pamela's ring,' I said.

'A good price? Oh, that ring belonged to my grandmother,' said Treat. 'It's been in the family. Didn't cost anything.'

'Didn't cost *you* anything, deputy,' I told Treat. 'Cost me a hundred bucks.'

***

At Holiday's, a backhoe had been brought in to dig a hole beside where the sugarhouse had stood. Eight or nine feet deep by ten long, it was more than big enough. In fact, I was surprised how little room the building took up when it was no longer a building but a pile of blackened rubble. Homer had taken the evaporator to save it. He'd taken the windows. He'd taken unbroken bricks from the fire arch. All that was left of the sugarhouse was dirty charcoal and rusty nails.

Homer and I sat in his truck and watched young Duncan March throw the burned lumber and roofing into the hole. Stripped to his waist, covered with sweat and soot, he went along steadily, lifting heavy timbers and other larger members from the pile, hefting them and tossing them down the hole. He had a long shovel for the loose spoil. We'd been there a couple of hours. Duncan had kept at it without a pause. He was tireless.

'Look at that kid go,' said Homer. 'Don't you wish you could still work like that?'

'Not really, no,' I said.

'Me, either,' said Homer.

Homer had hired the backhoe on his own dime. Not nothing, but he wanted to get things cleaned up before the musicians from Boston showed up for the summer. He hoped they would make it good. He thought they would; though he knew they weren't going to like losing their building.

'The musical gals are going to be ripped,' said Homer.

'Not at you,' I said. 'It wasn't your fault.'

'No,' said Homer. 'Guess I'll lay it off on those two from down-country.'

'Lay it off on Big John,' I said.

'Good idea,' said Homer. 'That's what I'll do.'

On the rubble pile, Duncan was taking a break. We watched him pull a bandanna from his rear pocket and mop his forehead, neck and chest.

'Kid's slowing down,' said Homer.

'He's about done it,' I said.

He about had. When Duncan had cleared as much of the burned-up waste as he could, he'd quit. Then the backhoe would come in again. He would use its blade to push the last of the rubble into the hole. Then he would fill the hole with dirt removed in digging it. It would mound the fill; maybe Homer would seed the mound to grass. That would be all. In a thousand years, ten thousand, it would be as though Holiday's sugarhouse had never existed.

***

'You know?' said Wingate. 'I've about decided you were right.'

'Can I get you to sign a paper on that?' I asked him. 'I'd like it to show it to Clemmie. She don't think I'm ever right.'

'No, sir,' said Wingate. 'Your married life's on you. I ain't about to interfere.'

'Right about what?' I asked him.

I was driving Wingate to the clinic for his checkup. He had gotten so he was barely able to walk, even with his cane. Besides that, he claimed, there was nothing wrong with him. He said he only went for his checkups to see who would turn up at the clinic. The cast of characters there interested Wingate.

'Doctor I saw last time?' said Wingate. 'Looked like he's about twelve? He's from India.'

'Is that right? What part?'

'Don't know,' said Wingate. 'Don't know what parts there are of India. Very nice young fellow. Talked like the King of England. Took plenty of time with me. Told me to go on doing whatever it was I was doing. I asked him what that was. He said he didn't know, but whatever it was, it seemed to work, me being still alive, and all. He said I could go on this way for years.'

'That's your plan, then, is it?'

'You bet,' said Wingate.

'What are you going to do with all that time?' I asked him.

'Going to work on local history,' said Wingate. 'Before it all gets lost and forgot. People have it all wrong. I did, myself. That's what I mean about your being right. That time we went into the woods at Metcalfs', Beer Hill, there, on the old road? We got as far as the slide. Right?'

'Okay,' I said.

'We ought to have gone in from the other end,' said Wingate. 'From Garlands', there. We ought to have gone in on the south side of the hill, not the north, like we did. We didn't pass Metcalfs'. Like you said, we never got to it.'

'I thought you said how you'd hunted all over that hill, going back years and years,' I said.

'So I have,' said Wingate.

'I thought you knew it, then.'

'So I do,' said Wingate. 'But the thing is, the old rememberer ain't what she used to be. I don't *forget*, exactly. Hell, no. I remember things just as clear? But I don't always remember where they belong, so to speak. I don't always remember which end of them to pick up. You know what I'm saying?'

'I ain't sure I do,' I said.

'You will,' said Wingate. 'And, then, another thing. I've more than hunted the valley, here. I've hunted the woods all over this end of the state, all my life. The woods? By and by, they get to look a lot alike.'

'You sound like Carlotta,' I told him.

'Who's Carlotta?'

'Lady friend of Addison's,' I said.

'Addison's? Oh, Lawyer Jessup, sure,' said Wingate.

'But, look,' I went on, 'talking about how all the woods start to look the same? Maybe it ain't the woods.'

'What else would it be?'
'Maybe it's you, getting older.'
'Me?' said Wingate.

***

Dwight Farrabaugh and I got ourselves settled into a booth at Humphrey's. Farrabaugh had business in the valley, he said. He offered to blow me to a doughnut. In fact, he was on a goodwill mission. He was mending fences. Not a moment too soon, either, as far as I was concerned.

Now Dwight looked around the room, high and low, and in the corners.

'I haven't been in here in a couple of years,' Dwight said. 'Something's different. What's different?'

He was right. Humphrey had overhauled his décor. Gone were Pearl Harbour, the World Trade Centre, the assassinations. At an estate sale up the valley, Humphrey had found a box of old *Saturday Evening Post* covers from the golden age, neatly framed and matted. Now, smiling schoolboys and girls, kindly doctors, teachers and policemen, happy families at Thanksgiving, at Christmas, happy dogs and cats – a whole peaceful, secure, contented world looked down from the same walls that had lately been devoted to death, destruction and man's inhumanity to man.

'Humphrey's swapped out his look,' I told Farrabaugh.

Dwight nodded. 'So he has,' he said.

'Like it?' I asked him.

'I don't know,' said Dwight. 'I guess the tourists do.'

'Speaking of tourists,' I said. 'I ain't heard anything about our two visitors from the other week: Mendez and Bray.'

'You mean O'Rourke and Schmidt?' Dwight asked.

'O'Rourke and Schmidt?'

'Their real names,' said Dwight. 'Correction: their *new* real names, the most recent names we had for them. There are probably others.'

'I ain't heard any more on them, by any name.'

'What did you expect to hear?'

'Where are they? Are they in custody? Do they have a court date?'

Dwight laughed. 'Court date? Why would they have a court date?'

'Ain't they going to be tried?'

'For what? Hell, no, they won't be tried. They'll be deported. We turned them over to Immigration, first thing. Where are they? I have no idea. Far away, I hope.'

'What about Armentrout, the lawyer? He set them on. He's the one you want. Is he far away, too?'

'He might as well be,' said Dwight. 'We looked into him right off. He's got a room full of witnesses putting him at a bar association conference in L.A. when you say he was up here doing evil.'

'So we all run around in circles and wind up with jack shit. Is that about it, Captain?'

'Wouldn't be the first time that's happened, would it?' said Dwight. 'Come on, Lucian, lighten up a little for me, here.'

'Wouldn't be the first time you came in and took over an investigation I had going, either,' I went. 'I don't appreciate that, Captain.'

Dwight laughed again. 'I know you don't, Lucian,' he said. I don't blame you. But, look: we've all got our jobs to do, don't we? We do the jobs we have, not the ones we don't, not somebody else's job. Okay?'

'No, it ain't okay,' I said.

'Good man,' said Dwight. 'You'll be fine. I've got to get going. Finish your doughnut.'

***

Carlotta, Addison and I stood at the edge of the big hayfield behind the inn and watched the sky to the south. With us was a kid from the inn to help with Carlotta's bags. It was nine in the morning. We were waiting for Carlotta's dust off. Her bags were packed and ready. She'd had her breakfast with Addison. Dinner she'd get in Paris. That's Paris, France.

'Keep an eye on this one won't you, Sheriff?' Carlotta asked me, pointing at Addison. 'I'm afraid he's going native.'

'What do you mean, *going*?' Addison asked her. 'I *am* native. Born in this house. On the kitchen table. It don't get more native than that.'

'*Don't* it?' Carlotta asked. 'Listen to you. But take care, darling. You know the old joke: just because the kittens were born in the oven doesn't make them biscuits. You used to speak English, at least. I mean, when were you last out of this valley?'

'Day before yesterday,' said Addison. 'Hah. How do you like that?'

'Where did you go?'

'Brattleboro.'

'And that's how far?'

'Ten miles, maybe not quite.'

'And the last time before that you'd been so far?'

'Don't recall,' said Addison.

'Q.E.D. darling, isn't it?' said Carlotta.

Addison laughed. 'All right, then, Lottie,' he said. 'You win. No biscuits here. Just accents. I wish you'd stick around, though. We might make a Vermonter out of you yet.'

Carlotta sniffed. 'I think not,' she said.

We looked up. With a thumping and beating on the air, a helicopter came into sight to the south. It cleared the trees and flew directly over us. It circled the hayfield once, then again, then it settled awkwardly to the ground. Its rotors slowed, stopped. The helicopter sat down on its skids, ungainly and strange, looking like a giant cricket or grasshopper with an eggbeater on its back.

'Well, then,' said Carlotta. She turned to embrace Addison and give me a little peck on the cheek. She picked up her light bag and started toward the helicopter. The boy followed her with the heavy bags in a wheelbarrow.

As Carlotta approached the helicopter, a forward door opened and a man wearing a helmet and a one-piece flight suit got down and opened his arms to Carlotta. She went to him, they hugged and held each other briefly. Then Carlotta climbed into the helicopter, the man following her. The doors closed. The helicopter's rotors began to turn heavily.

'Carlotta knows the pilot, I guess,' I said.

'That's not the pilot,' said Addison.

I looked again. In the side window, to the pilot's right, the man in the flight suit turned and looked across the field, toward us. He was looking at me. I thought I saw him nod. I didn't nod back. I wanted him gone. He was no friend of mine, and he, his money, his power, his friends, his life had no place in my valley.

Then the helicopter stirred, tilted forward and lifted off. Its wind beat against our faces. The kid from the inn had rejoined us. He was excited. 'Never saw one of those before up close,' he told us. 'Fucking hoot, right?'

Addison glanced at him, then at me. He raised his eyebrows and shook his head.

'I'm going to have me one of those someday,' said the kid.

'I don't doubt it,' said Addison. The three of us stood and watched Rex Lord and his passengers rise, gain altitude, turn into their course and disappear over the treetops.

Envoi

Clemmie wound the shoulder strap of her nightgown around a finger and tugged it up a little. She slid her bottom back toward the headboard of our bed so she could get sitting right, with the builder's drawings propped against her knees. She pushed her glasses up off the end of her nose. 'Right here,' she said. 'And here, and here, and here.'

'Yes,' I said. I lay on my back beside Clemmie.

'Those are the footings,' said Clemmie. 'They're concrete tubes. Rory says we'd probably need four more, these are just what he drew.'

'Four, eight, what the hell?' I said. Under the covers, Clemmie poked me in the side.

'How many guys does Rory say?' I asked Clemmie.

'Three.'

'Oh, come on,' I said. 'Same thing: three ain't much of a show. You'd better tell Rory six, seven, at least.'

Clemmie ignored that. She didn't poke me, she didn't jump to the red line, she didn't pick up a missile. She had other things on her mind. Plus, she hadn't anything good to throw just then. She shuffled Rory's plans and showed me a second sheet laying out posts, plates, rafters, and the rest.

'See?' Clemmie asked.

'That ain't a deck,' I said. 'That's a porch.'

'Right. Rory says once you've got your footings, your sills, it's just as easy to go ahead up. Then you roof it, and you've got a real porch. Much nicer than a deck. And easy? Nothing to it, Rory says.'

'Course Rory says it. He ain't paying for it.'

'Neither are you,' said Clemmie.

'I'm not? Who is?'

'Daddy said he'd like to give us the porch as an anniversary present.'

'Our anniversary's in March,' I said.

'So, shall I tell him no, thanks?'

'I didn't say that. Let me think it over.'

'Okay,' said Clemmie. 'Think fast, though, right?'

'Now you mention it,' I said. 'I wouldn't mind having a good place where I could sit and work on my memoirs.'

'You're writing your memoirs?' Clemmie asked me.

'I will be.'

'When?'

'Starting right after the next election,' I said.

Clemmie put her hand tenderly on my chest. 'Come on, honey,' she said. 'You're still down about Evelyn, that's all. You'll win the next election, the same as you've won the others. Everybody knows you. Everybody trusts you. Everybody likes you.'

'Not everybody,' I said.

Clemmie let Rory's drawings slide from her lap and rustle to the floor beside the bed. She took off her glasses and put them aside. She punched her pillows and shifted herself down so she was lying closer. She turned to me.

'Sure, they do,' she said. 'And, besides, who else would they get?'

'There's your question,' I told her.

Also Available

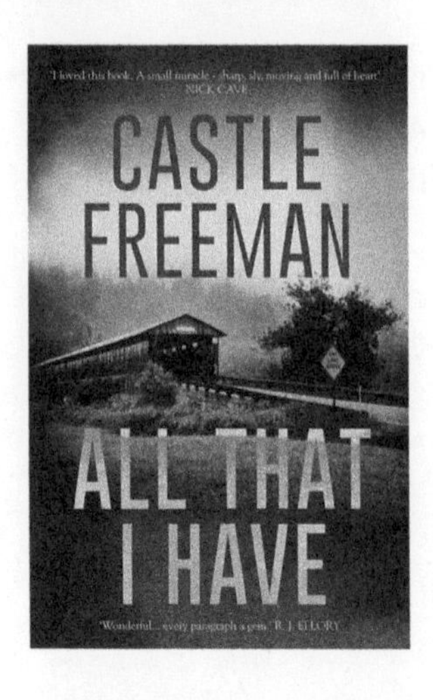

Lucian Wing is an experienced, practical man who enforces the law in his corner of Vermont with a steady hand and a generous tolerance. But when local tearaway Sean 'Superboy' Duke starts to get tangled up with a group of major league Russian criminals, things start to go awry in the sheriff's small, protected domain.

With an ambitious and aggressive deputy snapping at his heels and a domestic crisis of his own to confront, Wing must call on all the personal resources he has cultivated during his working life: patience, tact, and – especially – humour.

Can Wing's low-key approach to law enforcement prevail?

Also Available

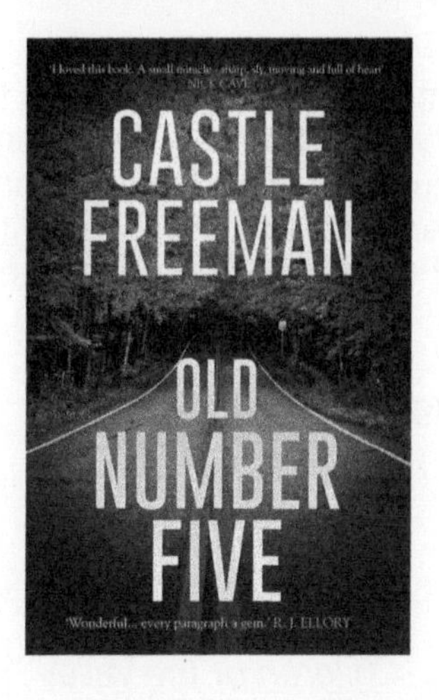

Lucian Wing is the sheriff of a backwoods county in Vermont, a hardscrabble place far from the picture-postcard gaze. He is also a man with a problem.

Multiple problems, in fact, including a threatening superior; a wandering wife; a hard-drinking father-in-law; a demented mother; a squad of deputies variously overzealous and moronic; a mysterious vigilante band operating in his jurisdiction; and a formidably bloodthirsty local carnivore…

Wing needs to draw on all his patience, knowledge and (especially) humour to resolve things. Not least, to honour the ancient rule that one ambiguous ally refers to as 'Old Number Five'.

About Castle Freeman's Novels

'Practically all the writing I have done – fiction, essays, history, journalism, and more – has been in one way or another about rural northern New England, in particular the State of Vermont, and the lives of its inhabitants, a source of unique and undiminishing interest, at least to me.'

The Lucian Wing novels –

All That I Have

Old Number Five

Children of the Valley

Other –

Go With Me

The Devil in the Valley

About the Author

Castle Freeman was born in 1944 in San Antonio, Texas. He was brought up on the South Side of Chicago, and later went to college in New York. In 1972, he moved with his wife to the southeastern corner of Vermont, where they have remained since.

He is an award-winning author not only of fiction, but also of personal essays, reporting, op-ed matter, history and natural history. He has been a regular contributor to several periodicals, including *The Old Farmer's Almanac* (1982–2011).

Note from the Publisher

To receive background material and updates on new releases by Castle Freeman, sign up at farragobooks.com/castlefreeman-signup